Sweet Honesty

Additional Titles
by Stephanie Perry Moore

Preteen
Carmen Browne Series
Book 1   True Friends

Teen
Payton Skky Series
Book 1   Staying Pure
Book 2   Sober Faith
Book 3   Saved Race
Book 4   Sweetest Gift
Book 5   Surrendered Heart

Laurel Shadrach Series
Book 1   Purity Reigns
Book 2   Totally Free
Book 3   Equally Yoked
Book 4   Absolutely Worthy
Book 5   Finally Sure

CARMEN BROWNE SERIES #2

Sweet Honesty

Stephanie Perry Moore

MOODY PUBLISHERS
CHICAGO

ISBN: 0-7394-6614-3
ISBN-13: 978-0-7394-6614-8

Printed in the United States of America

To my other mothers

Elva Barksdale

Hazel Randall

and

Marcella Williams

You were the major part of the village that raised me.
Thanks for taking me under your wing and always
honestly telling me what I needed to hear to be better.
More folks need to love on our children as you did for me.
I pray you're proud.

Contents

Acknowledgments   8
1. Soft Tone   11
2. On Key   23
3. Perfect Harmony   41
4. Deaf Ear   55
5. Loud Noise   71
6. Dope Sound   87
7. Indoor Voice   103
8. Listen More   119
9. Simply Right   135

Acknowledgments

I should be satisfied. God has blessed me to be a wife, author, and mother of two spunky, yet adorable girls. However, deep inside I long to adopt a child who needs a family. I guess I feel I've been blessed with so much that I want to spread that love to a kid who has no hope. Feeling like it will never happen, I was sad.

However, I kneeled down in prayer and poured my heart out to God. After my honesty session, He revealed to me that I've got to be happy with what I have. Maybe one day He'll add to my family, or maybe He won't. Either way, I've got to rejoice. Also, the Lord showed me that maybe He planted this longing to adopt in my heart, so that I could write this novel to share with young people that kids in foster care are special too.

See, it doesn't matter whether you are in a stable two-parent home, being raised by a hardworking single parent, or in a foster home feeling alone—always know Jesus loves all the little children of the world equally. He hears you when you call. Honestly come to Him and tell Him what's on your heart. He cares. What a sweet feeling!

And here's a special thanks to all those who care deeply for my writing.

To my parents, Dr. and Mrs. Franklin D. Perry Sr., your honesty has refined me along the way. Thanks for teaching me every day is a great day.

To Moody Publishers' Lift Every Voice line, particularly Lori Wenzinger, you made sure my marketing material was top notch. Thanks for working extra hard.

To Bethany Christian Services, Atlanta Branch, all you do blesses many. Serving on your board adds more purpose to my life.

To my upbeat girls, Sydni and Sheldyn—boy, you guys can argue sometimes. Learn from this book to always be sweet to each other.

To my husband, DCM, you serve so many with your ministry. I am so proud of the heart you have.

To my dear preteen readers, hoping this novel teaches you that honesty is the best policy. Remember to daily strive to please God.

And to my Savior, honestly, I just want to make a difference for You. Help me want only what you want for me. And may each reader desire the same.

1

Soft Tone

This is the worst Christmas I've ever had in my ten years of life," I said honestly, stating how I felt to my adorable brown teddy bear, Budgie, as I went on pretending he could talk back. "What are you sayin'? Excuse me? It wasn't that bad? Yeah, right. We didn't leave the house the whole day. It was supposed to be family time, quiet time, just the five Browne family members time. Today made twenty-four hours seem like sixty. The only good thing about this Christmas is now it's nine o'clock, and soon Christmas will be over and my friends will be back home. Then I can start another day."

"Carmen, honey," my mom said as she talked to me on the other side of my closed door, "your dad and I are heading downstairs to watch a movie. You want to join us?"

"No, thanks," I uttered, sounding sort of pitiful as I looked down at my bear. "I just want to spend time with you, Budgie."

"Carmen, who are you talking to, hon?" my mom asked, obviously able to make out part of my quiet voice.

I know I wasn't headed to college or anything, but I thought myself to be pretty grown-up. I was in fifth grade, after all, ruling my new elementary school; but as I looked down at the stuffed animal that I had spent the last few minutes having a pity party with, I realized that I was still just a kid. But I couldn't let my mom know that I was talking to the bear.

When I stalled and didn't answer the question she said, "Oh, you and Budgie are talking, huh. I'm so glad Cassie found him for you. Well, relax, sweetie, you know we love you. And it's okay to still talk to your bear."

"I love you too, Mom," I said with a big smile on my face, happy, feeling good that she made me feel good about me being me.

I had been looking for Budgie ever since we moved to Ettrick, Virginia. The place was okay, but it was nothing like Charlottesville. I missed my best friend, Jillian Gray, though. We were different in skin color, but we thought a lot alike.

I couldn't be too down about her because my parents always taught me that God knew how to take care of His own. He gave me two new friends in this mostly black town, though today I couldn't talk to them. I had left Layah, my tomboyish girlfriend, and Riana, my little shy buddy, several messages; and neither one of them had called me back.

My little sister, Cassie, had annoyingly been in and out of my room several times. The only time I cared was when she brought me my Christmas present, my Budgie. He was packed away in one of her stuffed animal boxes, and since she had four boxes, the one with Budgie was just recently opened.

"I know you missed me," I said as I squeezed his ears, knowing I missed him too.

The day really was boring because, though we were all there, we didn't really spend time together. Dad was home the whole day, but he was watching football. He wanted my brother, Clay, to join him. Clay did but was there in body only. My brother wasn't as much of a sports nut as my dad, and, well, they weren't getting along at all. My mom spent most of her time in the kitchen fixing breakfast, lunch, dinner, and cleaning in between.

Since I went to the grocery store so many times with Mom, helped her prepare all the food, and wrapped a bunch of gifts for her before Christmas, I didn't have to clean up the kitchen this time. Thankfully, it was Cassie's job. So that left me alone dialing my friends' numbers over and over again. Not once did they call me back.

"Oh, Budgie, I guess it's just me and you. Let me see what else can I tell you," I said, sounding quite pitiful.

All of a sudden, I heard the greatest sound. The phone was ringing. Quickly, I picked it up so that Cassie wouldn't get it since the phone was in the hall, but I should have known she heard it. She was talking before I could say hello.

"Who's calling for her?" she asked, being a pest.

"Cassie!" Riana yelled out, "is your sister there?"

"Maybe," my sister said, still not bending.

Layah chimed in on the three-way call. "Silly. Get your sister."

Pumped to hear from my girls, I said nicely to my little sister, "Cassie, I've got it. Please hang up the phone."

I was so excited to hear my girlfriends' voices that it never dawned on me that I didn't hear a click from my little eight-year-old pest of a sister.

I was just talkin' until Riana said, "I think someone else is still on the phone."

"Okay, then, good night, y'all," Cassie said in a sassy way before hanging up the phone from trying to eavesdrop.

"I've been calling you guys all day. This was the worst Christmas. Where have y'all been?" I asked, whining.

"Oh, did somebody miss us?" Riana said, teasing me. "Now you get a chance to see what it's like."

"Yep, she's the one always on the go, leaving us bored at home," Layah said.

I looked over at Budgie and rolled my eyes. My friends knew me well, which was really cool. *Plus, I thought to myself, a true friend would be happy that their friends were having a good Christmas, but yet I wanted them to be bored at home like me. That wasn't right.*

"Okay, I'm sorry," I said, looking up, then turning away from my bright light. "I'm glad you guys were out and all."

"Don't sweat it. We're glad you care," Layah said.

Hearing that, I smiled. The light in my room bothered me, so I quickly turned it off. Then I nestled under my covers to talk more with my friends. I was so happy to be on the line with them. I tucked Budgie into bed so he could sleep. I didn't need to talk to him anymore.

"Girrrl, we're got the perfect plan," Layah said, sorta scaring me.

"Yes, it's really good. I'm nervous, but it's really good," Riana agreed, scaring me even more.

"Well, what is it, you guys? Just tell me!" I demanded.

"I'm about to tell you," Layah said. "Here it goes. Remember how we are always saying that we are really grown and we don't need to be babied by our parents?"

"Yeah, yeah," I hurried her.

"Okay, one weekend, like in the next month or two, we are going to plan to go to the mall," Layah said in a quiet tone as if she was saying top secret info.

"I'm not getting it. We've been hanging at the mall

together with our folks. What's so grown up about that?" I asked.

Layah went into a sly voice. "Good question. Here comes the good part: We'll have one parent dropping us off to another parent that will stay with us at the mall. But there won't be a parent there. We'll be alone."

That sounded really crazy to me. We couldn't lie. No way I was gonna go for that. Besides, how would we get home?

Layah continued as if she knew what I was thinking. "And we'll get home by telling a parent what time to pick us up, because the one they think will be with us will have to go somewhere other than home. They'll know all this before we go. Cool, huh?"

I waited then said, "Won't that be like lying to our parents? Come on, guys, we can't do that. We've got to rethink the plan."

"No, see, we knew you would say that," Layah voiced in a firm way. "How are we ever going to grow up if we don't take risks to show we are responsible? We've got to take a chance if we want them to see we can handle stuff. Are you a part of the threesome or not? The boys would do it, and that's why I always hang with boys. You guys threw a skirt on me, invited me to tea parties; now I want to be friends with you and do something a little adventurous, and you want to wimp out. And, Riana, you're not saying anything. Forget it."

I hit my pillow. I didn't want Layah not to hang with

us anymore. We'd come so far with our friendship over the last few months.

"Okay, okay, okay, I'm in. Let's do it," I said as I heard yells through the phone. "But we've got to have every detail down; my mom is smart. I'm not trying to get caught. She did tell me I could get a cell phone when I get responsible. I'm down to show her that I am."

We talked a little longer, and though the plan was way out there, I was excited about my friends. Though the whole lying thing made me uneasy, I thought I could tell a "little fib" to gain my parents' trust and be really cool with my friends. I was still new around here. I couldn't let Layah and Riana down yet.

Before we hung up the phone, the three of us agreed to stick to the plan. We said we'd work out the details and aim to make our parents proud. I hoped it was going to work.

✪

After the call was over, Budgie told me that he had to go to the bathroom. Oh, well, that wasn't true. I had to go. Though the clock said ten, I wasn't really sleepy, probably 'cause I'd laid around in bed all day.

I stopped before I got there. I bumped into the wall because it was dark. I didn't want to wake anybody up. Then I heard a weird noise coming from my brother's room. However, I thought I shouldn't go in and investigate

17

because I knew Clay could take care of himself. He'd probably just go off on me for caring, so why even bother?

Then I tried to walk back to my room in the darkness. However, I couldn't pass Clay's door this time without going in. I was sure the funny noise was him crying.

I opened up the door and said in a soft, concerned voice, "Are you okay?"

When my brother didn't answer, I turned to try and walk away but went back anyway.

"Clay, listen, I know you think of me as your nagging little sister and if you don't want me in here, I don't care. I know I don't say it all the time, but I love you. I've never heard you cry like this."

I stood still, waiting for him to open up. He didn't. I couldn't give up.

"Clay, did you and Dad argue or something? What's going on? You're scaring me."

"I'm all right," he said, sniffling to try and dry up his tears.

I walked in the dark only a few steps before tripping. Walking a little more toward his voice, I thought I had a clear path, but leave it to my brother to have his skateboard in the way. I tripped over it, fell on the bottom part of his bed, and hurt my toe badly.

"Ouch!" I screamed.

"You okay?" Clay rushed over to me and asked with deep concern.

Smiling I said, "See, you care about me too."

"Were you acting?" he said, lightly hitting me with his pillow.

"No, I wasn't. My foot hurts. That stupid skateboard. Mom told you to put that thing in the closet."

"No one was supposed to be in my room. I knew it was in the middle of the floor." My brother went on talking to me like normal. Then he blurted out, "You know Dad and I, we just don't get along. I'll click more with my real dad. I want to find my family."

There was silence between us. His words hurt. Why was he saying those things? "Carmen, can you understand that for a minute?" he asked before crying again.

I didn't understand it. Though we had just recently found out that he was adopted, he was my brother and no other family mattered. Yet he was just crying so badly that it hurt me that he was hurting. Since he said that he wanted to find his family, then I had to put my feelings aside and help.

"How could parents give their children away?" he said.

"Different things happen to people, Clay. I don't know why all the stuff that happens does. I do understand being a little bummed out about it, though. God showed me that He knew what He was doing when we moved and He worked everything out. And just know He's going to show you why you're better off with us. I'm happy it worked out this way."

"What do you mean you're happy?" my brother asked in an upset voice.

"Because, Clay, if it didn't happen, then you wouldn't be my brother. Who'd nag me and who would help me with the computer? And who'd understand Cassie getting on my nerves? Only you. I'm happy you're here."

"I hear ya. I'm really sad that my parents didn't love me enough to keep me. I got to find them, Sis. I want them to look me in the eye and tell me they don't want me. I know my real dad won't be able to do that. Can't you see, Sis?" he asked.

I could not join him in imagining the happy union. If he moved away I didn't know what I'd do. He asked me if I would keep his secret that he wanted to meet his parents to myself. I agreed to honor his wishes and we said good night.

When I got back to my room, I just prayed, "Lord, please help Clay be happy with this family. And if that's not supposed to be how it goes, help me find peace with him leaving us. Also, I'm so sorry I thought today was the worst Christmas ever. Guess sometimes I'm really selfish. I just wanted today to be about me getting a whole bunch of things. Me having so much fun with my friends—the focus all on me and not on You and Your Son's birthday. Please forgive me. In Jesus' name, amen."

✪

The next day, I helped Mom with the waffle maker. Pouring the batter through all the little grooves was kinda cool. I just push it down for a minute and when it beeps, I let it up . . . presto, perfect waffles!

I was really caught off guard when she said, "So, Miss Lady, I heard you talking when I passed your room last night. Your girlfriends called you back, huh?"

I slowly nodded, hoping she didn't hear what I was planning with them. "Yes, ma'am."

"And what had you laughing so?" she asked.

With excitement I said, "We're planning a sleepover and outing at the mall."

I could have stuffed my mouth with the waffles I was making. I didn't mean to tell her what I'd just hoped she didn't hear. I didn't have any details, and I knew she was going to ask a ton of questions.

So I said, "Before you ask me anything, we haven't planned it all out yet."

"That's fine. I wasn't trying to get all the information now just as long as you have everything in place later. Set the waffles on the table and get the orange juice out too, please, honey. A slumber party sounds great. I trust you to make the plans. And I can go with you all to the movies. Let me know. See, moving wasn't a bad thing, after all, was it?"

I smiled. Though I had laid the foundation with my mom, deep down I felt bad, knowing I wasn't telling her the whole truth. I had left out the most important part that she would say no to . . . going to the mall without parents. What had I agreed to?

To make me feel worse, my mom came over and threw her arms around me, gave me a big kiss on the cheek, and told me she was proud of me. I felt so close to her. Seemed like I could talk to her about anything . . . well, anything except our plan and boys.

She said, "I love you dearly. Just keep doing the right thing. Let the Holy Spirit guide you."

Biting my lip, I once again started second-guessing myself. Mom asked me to get the rest of the family for breakfast.

"Am I letting the Holy Spirit guide me?" I asked myself in a soft tone.

2

On Key

"Fifty-eight, fifty-nine," I counted with my arms in the air so that Riana and Layah would know when to yell out with me. "Now!"

"Happy New Year!" the three of us said together as we drank some sparkling grape juice from my mom's fancy crystal goblets. I didn't have the refreshing, fizzy stuff often, but when I did I loved it.

"Let's all say what we want this year," Layah said in her bossy tone.

We'd already talked all night, so I didn't want to talk more. Plus, I was so tried. I was happy my friends were staying over, and at first I wanted to be up all night. However, my body was pooped. I looked at them with a disapproving glare. Layah rolled her eyes. I knew she wanted me to do what she requested. And these were my guests, so whatever they wanted to do I decided to tough it out and be down for.

This impromptu sleepover turned out to be a great idea. I was so tired because my day was so much fun. We giggled all day looking in fashion magazines and modeling our new Christmas clothes. We really had a deep conversation talking about things that were bothering each of us. I didn't want my friends to have drama like me, but it was nice to know I wasn't the only ten-year-old going through things. It came out that we all had family issues. But we vowed to be there for each other.

Layah talked first. "I used to like wearing boy clothes. But now I really want to change. And I appreciate you guys saying you will help me get a little stylish. I'm getting older now and some of that cute stuff you both wear I like a lot. This year, I want to be more into fashion."

Riana and I smiled at her. Next it was Riana's turn. She laughed and laughed. Layah gave her the eye, like *come on*. When Riana giggled in my direction, I motioned for her to hurry up.

"I think I want my bad feelings for boys to change," Riana barely uttered before busting out with another laugh.

"Yuck," Layah said. "Who cares about them?"

I pointed to myself and quickly gave Riana a high five. Layah just shook her head in disappointment. Riana and I so admired that Layah got to hang with the boys we liked all the time because of her cool athletic abilities. She could beat all of them at everything. Riana liked a bad boy in our class, and I liked Spencer, or Spence, as we called him, the shy guy who happened to be the grandson of my dad's boss.

Layah didn't understand where Riana was coming from, but I said, "I hear you, friend."

"Quit fooling around," Layah said, sorta irritated with Riana and me.

"Okay, my turn," I said in a silly way. "I want us to continue being there for each other."

"We don't do that," Layah said to me as if what I said was so dumb.

"Yes, we do," I said with a little frustration in my voice. "Earlier today we talked about so much. We were honest with each other and really shared our feelings."

"No, we didn't," Layah said, still being difficult.

"Yeah, Layah, we did," I challenged. "You were all sad talking about your dad dating again. We listened and then made you realize that you'll always be number one in your dad's eyes, remember."

She started smiling. "You're right!"

"And, Riana, you said how you felt bad because your aunt and uncle might be splitting up. Layah told you to keep praying and maybe they'll work it out. Only a true friend could really be there and listen like that. You haven't thought about your family any more today."

Riana nodded her head, and I got real close to both of them and said, "I just wanted to drink my juice and go to sleep, but you guys kept making me stay up and get over myself and help me enjoy this whole thing. I love you guys."

"Oh, Carmen," Riana said. "Group hug."

I leaned in to Riana and then I turned toward Layah. She was cool but wasn't down for the hug and all. I gave her a puppy-dog look.

"It's getting a little too mushy," Layah yelled out, before giving in and hugging us anyway.

At 1:10 a.m. we finally settled down. I was so glad my two friends brought their own sleeping bags, because my full-sized bed wasn't big enough for the three of us. When we slept in my bed, Layah was in the middle and, boy, was she sleeping wild. She kicked Riana and me off of the sides. And when we both ended up on the floor, we woke Layah up and pulled her down with us, and we made our bed on the floor. Then we were all able to drift off to sleep.

The next morning before breakfast we went over our plans for the mall-shopping trip. My conscience was bothering me kinda bad. I had to tell myself that we were going to do this for a good reason. We wanted to prove to our parents that we were responsible. A little fib to get that point across to them was okay, I told myself.

The rest of the morning was so much fun; I had my friends help me make waffles. It wasn't until Layah put a little too much dough into the mix and had to throw her whole bowl out that things got really funny. Riana tried to help her make another batch, but hers was too watery. So I just had them sit there and watch me work.

I was happy that my brother and sister were down at Riana's house. Riana and I still couldn't believe our families had siblings the same ages. I not only made breakfast for my friends, but for my parents too. See, that was part of the plan. We agreed to do really well in school, do extra chores at home, and just be really perfect so that our parents wouldn't even question our plans to go to the mall.

Yep, we had it figured out pretty good. I was still scared a little of lying, though. I hoped I'd soon become totally confident in the plan. I was tired of second-guessing myself.

★

"Mom, it's just not right," I whined in a pitiful tone, hoping that my sad voice would make her let me go shopping. My mom was a volunteer with an organization called the Family Alternative. They educated potential parents on the benefits of adoption. "I don't understand why I have to go to this adoption thing. I mean, why don't you take Cassie? Mom, she loves to play hostess; why me? Grandma sent me some money, and I just want to get a few more things before school starts back next week. Please, Mom? I don't wanna go."

I could tell I was sorta getting on my mom's last nerve, as she sometimes said. This time she didn't say it; she just sorta looked out the window up to the sky as if she was asking God to give her the strength not to lose it with me. So I settled down and decided not to push.

"Carmen, I really need you to help me today," my mother said, getting her coat out of the hall closet. "I've been asked to be a board member for this adoption agency. And today is an awareness meeting and luncheon for people interested in learning more about adoption. You're old enough to do community service. You'll be very helpful."

"Me help somebody with adoption, huh? Mom, you're not making any sense," I said, sitting on the steps looking pitiful. "Clay's the adopted one. How can I help?"

"There will be parents there with their biological children. The families are considering adopting and want to have their children interact with kids like you so that they can find out from a child's point of view how adoption affects a family. Maybe you could talk to those kids and tell them something that might make them really excited about the whole adoption process. I don't know. I just know God can use you to help me today," she said, making me feel bad that I didn't want to do it.

My mom always saw so much in me. Definitely stuff I never saw in myself. I thought she was completely wrong. Two hours later, I was sitting with four kids from different families. Some were not excited about their parents considering adoption. I was surprised about how much I did know on the subject. I knew the stuff that mattered to them. When I made the statement that a kid who doesn't share the same blood as the ones already in the home can have a bond, the questions started.

A girl whose mom was thinking about adopting an older sister asked, "Well, because she's not my sister, how can I feel like she's my sister? How can I welcome her? How can I make her feel comfortable?"

Thinking of my bond with Clay I said, "I think all that's going to come naturally. Just be who you are and let her be who she is, and believe you guys will become close. You don't have to force it. I have a sister—a blood sister—who is two years younger than me and, trust me, I would trade her in for an adopted sister any day."

They laughed, knowing that I wasn't serious. However, it proved my point that it didn't matter whether a brother or sister was adopted or biological; in reality, only love matters.

A boy with red hair and freckles asked, "My parents are thinking about a little boy who is on medicine or something. Won't that be bad?"

"I can't tell you anything about that. But I know if your parents are considering him, they'll be able to handle it. My brother who is adopted has flaws just like me. But even with all of them put together I still don't want to ever give him back." I actually got really sad as I thought about Clay wanting to leave.

I talked with the other kids a little while longer. When we left our session, they told me they were ready to share their parents with a child who didn't have any because of our positive discussion. In the car with my mom on the way home, we talked about everything that was said.

"See, I knew God could use you," she told me as she gave me a wink.

I winked back as we pulled into the mall. I was glad I was honest with my mother and told her why I didn't want to go to the adoption luncheon. She helped me to see that I could benefit from being there. What a blessing. Now I could be blessed even more and buy some school clothes. And I couldn't wait to prove her wrong about me shopping without her. She'd see.

★

School had been in for a week. It was a new semester and instead of taking P.E., we would be taking music. I loved to sing, but I hadn't really sung since we'd moved. I just didn't feel like joining the church choir or singing the songs on the radio. When my teacher told us that we were going to music class, I got so excited. I liked that so much better than P.E. In P.E. it was almost like I was a fish out of water. I wasn't good at softball, kickball, volleyball, or any kind of ball. But music was definitely my thing.

As we walked down to the music room, Spence was be-

hind me. I could tell something was on his mind. I wanted
to turn around and ask what was up, but our teacher
strictly informed us to be quiet. The last thing I wanted to
do was start the year off on the teacher's bad list.

My teacher, Miss Pryor, was getting ready for a wedding. Our P.E. teacher, Mr. DuBois, proposed to her last
year. I knew the wedding was going to be something special. Weddings were sweet. I remember when my sister
and I were flower girls in my aunt's wedding.

"Hey, Carmen," Spence said in a whisper, "don't turn
around or we'll get in trouble. Can you keep a secret?"

I nodded without saying a word.

He continued, "I hate I don't get to see you at games
anymore. We had fun."

That is so sweet, I thought to myself.

*He missed seeing me on weekends even though he sees me
Monday through Friday.* Maybe he thought I was extra cool
too. When we got to music class I sat with my girls.

"Hello, boys and girls. I am Ms. Hastings, your music
teacher. Come in and take a seat. Our school got a grant,
and we have many new things."

There were all kinds of instruments around the room.
Drums, bells, tambourines. I could tell everyone was in
awe.

There were four fifth grade classes. Two of us had P.E.
last semester and two of us had music. The music class
had gone on and on about how much they liked music.
They had a Christmas concert, and those singing sounded

great and those playing instruments sounded good too. We were all very excited that it was our turn. None of the boys wanted to sing. They all wanted to play instruments, and they went rushing to grab some.

"No instruments today, guys," Ms. Hastings said. "I asked you to sit down. You have to follow instructions."

She was really cool. She was around the same age as our teacher but instead of having brown skin with medium-length hair, she was a little darker with a short, sassy haircut. Layah really liked that because Ms. Hastings looked like her. And the clothes she had on were tight.

When Ms. Hastings stepped out into the hall to talk to the teacher, my friends leaned in so that we could talk.

"What was Spence talking about in the hallway?" Riana quizzed.

"Yeah, give us the 411," Layah seconded.

"You guys are so silly," I said, trying to play it off, but clearly something was on my mind. "Spence misses seeing me at the college football games," I told them.

The three of us giggled.

"Wait until I talk to him," Layah said harshly.

"No, you can't!" I yelled out.

Everyone in the class looked at me, wondering what I could have possibly been talking about. They couldn't tell him; he'd be angry. I hadn't keep my word to him.

In a softer tone I said, "Nobody can know. It was supposed to be between him and me. I shouldn't have told you guys. Now I feel horrible."

"Yep 'cause I want to know why Hunter hasn't said anything sweet to me."

"Riana, you can't mention it to him either. Promise me you . . ."

Just then, Ms. Hastings came back in and class went on. Though Riana and Layah had given me their word, I was really paranoid because I had also given Spence my word, and I had just told the secret. What made me think that they wouldn't do the same? If he ever found out . . . I dreaded the thought of it. Our friendship would definitely be over before it really began. I would have no one to blame but myself and all because I couldn't keep my big mouth shut. I could only hope I wouldn't regret it.

★

The week had gone by and we were on our way back to music class. Spence was behind me once again. This whole week had been weird. It was like he was avoiding me. I had a bad feeling of what that meant.

I quickly whispered, "Spence? Spence?"

"What, Carmen?" he answered back in a harsh tone.

A lump came into my throat, but I had to find out why he had changed. What had I done? As if I didn't know.

Before I could say anything he got pushed from the back into me.

"Ouch!" I said.

"Hunter, what are you doing?" Spence asked him.

"I just thought you wanted to hug your girlfriend so I pushed you into her."

A couple of boys in the class laughed. I could tell he was humiliated. I didn't know if it was Layah or Riana who had told, but somebody sure had. What he felt for me was nothing nice any longer.

"Spence, I'm sorry."

"Yeah, I bet you are. I asked you to keep a secret and you couldn't. Now I'm the big joke of the class. I thought you were different from all of these girls, but you are just like them. All of y'all talk too much."

He quickly raised his hand and asked if he could go to the bathroom. I wanted to cry. He thought I was like everyone else. He thought I was now just a regular, ordinary girl with a big mouth. Whether it was true or not, it didn't matter. What mattered to me was the boy that used to like me now didn't like me at all.

Sitting in music class Ms. Hastings played, "You've Got a Friend in Me." She could really sing. At that moment I didn't feel like I had a friend in anybody. I didn't know if I could trust Layah or Riana, and the one guy that I had been starting to understand was changing.

"I need you guys to sing on key. We're going to sing the first part, 'You've got a friend in me, you've got a friend in me.' I'm going to break you up into first soprano, second soprano, alto, tenor, and bass."

Last week Ms. Hastings had told me that I had a really nice voice, so she put me in second soprano. That meant that I could either go really high or really low. But today I just didn't feel like singing.

"No, Carmen, that's not the right key. I need you to listen to the piano and sing the note I play."

Though she played it three times so I could clearly get it, I sang it wrong three times. One would think I was tone-deaf. I really wasn't concentrating on the music. I could only replay the scene in the hall. What a mess I had made of things.

It was now Saturday and I hadn't talked to Riana or Layah. They tried to talk to me after school. They tried calling me on three-way the night before. I told my sister to tell them that I was asleep. One of them or both of them had betrayed me, and I wasn't up to finding out which one. I didn't want to hear anything they had to say. I moved to Ettrick without friends, and if I didn't have any it would be just fine with me. I made up my mind that I was going to be a singer, and I would concentrate on my career without any girlfriends.

Being honest with myself, I did miss them, though. But as my auntie taught me, *Do me wrong once, shame on you. Do me wrong twice, shame on me.* I wasn't going to let them get close enough to do me wrong again.

★

My family was now headed to the Super Bowl. It was going to be in the Washington Redskins' stadium. It was the Broncos against the Cowboys. I didn't care for either team. Since we had to come, I tried to enjoy my family.

My mom said this was so much fun since we weren't babies anymore. We went on tours of the Washington Monument and the White House. It actually was good to be in a different place.

When my dad used to play for the Redskins, he'd made quite a few friends on the team. He had kept in touch with many of them. And my mom missed all their wives that she was friends with. Their old buddies were all doing so many different things. One, in particular, owned a gospel record company. I was really pumped when my dad said we could go and tour his studio and drop Mom off there for a little gathering with his wife and some of their other old friends.

There was a group there called Pure Grace. They were three college girls from Howard University, another historically black college, like Virginia State where my dad coached. They could really sing. I sat there in the twirling chair listening to them. Every note they sang sounded great to my ears. I wanted to be just like them. Their music had such nice beats and such deep meaning.

"I see you're into our music," one of them said to me.

Smiling I said, "Yeah, you guys sound really good."

"What grade are you in?" she asked.

"Fifth."

"Do you like to sing?"

"Yeah."

"We saw you singing the chorus. Why don't you come back here and sing on the mic."

"Mom, can I?"

"Sure," my mom said before heading across the hall to a dinner with her friends.

I jumped out of the chair, grabbed a headset, and was ready for my turn.

"You sound good," another one said to me after I had messed around a bit.

"So, Charles," Mr. Perriman said to my dad, "your daughter has got some voice. We're always looking for new groups."

Boy, was I excited. He showed us the rest of the place. We went by the room down the hall, which had place settings for four. Mrs. Perriman and the other two ladies came running to the door to see Mom. They were really sweet, but I was tired of my cheeks being squeezed. They were all set for the game. Food, fellowship, and a big screen TV made me want to stay with them.

My mom told them she'd be right back as we continued on our tour of the place. Mr. Perriman started talking to my mom about her artwork. He was explaining how he wanted to do something different with the album cover for Pure Grace.

My mom asked, "Do you have a photo of them? I could do some sketches or something."

"That would be great, Claire. Hook it up and I'll pay you later. You know my money is good," he joked.

"Yeah, I know. You used to be a big spender back in the day," she laughed back and said.

When we got back to the room where we started, it was time for my brother, sister, and me to go with my dad. The group was still recording and I really didn't want to leave. I couldn't stop looking in awe at all three of them. Mr. Perriman had to know what I was thinking because he said, "You know Carmen is welcome to stay if she wants."

"Carmen, do you want to stay here with me?" my mom asked.

"Oh, please, Mama, please."

Mr. Perriman turned to my dad and said, "Charles, my sound guy would love to go to the Super Bowl with us. Let the girl stay. I'll buy her ticket."

My parents gave each other eye movements. I knew they were discussing me staying or going. They had a language all their own.

"Okay," my dad said, giving me a bear hug. "Carmen, you can stay. And, man, you don't have to buy the ticket. You're blessing us as well by letting her sit in on the session."

Once the game crew left, my mom made sure I knew to be good. She was just two doors down and said she'd check on me. I was so pumped to stay.

It took no time for the older girls and me to bond. They were treating me like their mascot. I had found out that their names were T.J., Mona, and Bianca.

"I wanna be in a group just like y'all," I said to them.

"We just sing for the Lord," Bianca said.

"Yeah, lifting our voices to Him comes so easy," T.J. replied. "We love the Lord."

"Is it easy being in a group? I think I might want to be a solo artist. My girlfriends can sing a little, but I can't trust them. That's what you've got to have in a girl group, right?"

They all looked at me as if I were wrong. Before any of them spoke, I thought about my friends, whom I'd missed dearly. Was I wrong?

"Don't misunderstand us," Mona said. "We don't always get along. I'm sure your girls are straight. Plus, if they did something, they need grace. In our group, we've got to not only have slammin' voices but also trust and respect for one another, much grace to give each other, and the love of the Lord. Many folks don't realize singing in a Christian group is much more than just singing on key."

3

Perfect Harmony

"Let me be clear, Carmen. Get things right with your friends," Mona encouraged. "We argue all the time. But we've come to understand that serving the Lord is more important than singing. So because of our relationship with Him, we have to love one another. Sometimes you have to let go of small stuff."

"Yep," T.J. explained. "Your friends might let you down, but nobody's perfect."

Bianca said, "And if you are thinking about singing professionally, it is going to be tough. You need good people around you. We are seniors at Howard, and we've been trying to do this music thing for three years. We have had producers who took advantage of us. We have also had bad managers. Just take your time, develop your craft, and keep singing for the Lord. Once you spend more time with Him, every aspect of your life will fall into place."

They gave me a lot to think about. The most important thing that I got from what they *didn't* say was if I wanted to sing for the Lord, I needed to know who Christ was in my life. If I was cool with Him, my life would be sweet.

Before they went back to singing I said, "Thanks for talking to me. I learned a lot. I'll be praying about mending things with my friends, and I really want to get to know God better. In my heart, I believe the song, 'Yes, Jesus Loves Me,' but I know I need to spend more time with Him."

Bianca said, "That's a good place to start, Carmen. Come sing with us."

I was honored they let me sing background on one of their songs. Only this time I wasn't messing around. They actually recorded it and said that if my parents approved they'd keep it on the album.

I told them that I knew their album wasn't out yet, but I was already their biggest fan. Anytime they were in Ettrick, they could count on me to tell folks to go see them, and I'd try to be the first one at the show.

"We will hold you to it," T.J. told me.

"If my parents say I can come, I'll be there for real. Y'all are great. I'm so glad I know you guys!" I shouted as if they were already famous.

"You'd better be glad you know Jesus," Mona said, patting me on the head.

"Yeah, you're right. And an awesome God led me to you guys."

Before it was time to go, they practiced some more. This time, not in the recording studio—they went down to the dance room and started choreographing their number. I was really excited because, even though it was gospel, it still had a beat. I had taken dance all my life, and, naturally, I always felt I had moves. Trying to keep up with the big girls proved that I had a lot to learn.

"Well, it's clear to us, li'l lady, that you are something special. You'll be our number one special fan," Mona said to me while pinching my cheeks.

I so wanted to not just be a little girl in their eyes. I wished I could be at all their rehearsals. But I knew that wasn't possible. So I settled on being cool with the fact that I had a special place in their hearts even though they had only known me for one day.

While we were driving back home that night, my brother and sister were knocked out. I just kept thinking back on my fabulous day. It was so late, but I just couldn't go to sleep. We couldn't spend the night at a hotel because the next day was a school day. I didn't even care who'd won the Super Bowl. I knew it wasn't as exciting as my studio time.

My dad saw me awake and said, "Carmen, you had better get some sleep. You've got school tomorrow and you'll have to be up early."

That was his nice way of saying, "Don't let me have to come and drag you out of bed in the morning."

"It seems like she wants to tell you all about her night. Maybe after she gets it out she will be able to go to sleep. It was exciting," my mom said to my father.

"Tell me," he asked. "Why are you so happy?"

"Daddy, they were great. That group is awesome. They let me sing with them."

"We heard you sing with them."

"But they let me record on their album."

"Yep. Charles," my mom said as if she was proud. "They want her on the album. I told them it was . . ."

"Did you say it was okay, Mom? Please say you said it was fine!" I asked in a panicked voice. "I was in the rest-room when they talked to you, and they wouldn't tell me what you said. You said yes, right?"

My mom said, "Calm down, girl. I told them they could keep your voice on the cut."

My dad said, "Go, girl. Plus, I hear you'll get a small check in the mail for it."

"Wow! Thanks for saying yes, and thanks for letting me stay with you. I really enjoyed myself."

"We are truly glad you had a good day. Every time I peeked in on you, your face was all smiles. I had fun too, but I think you had the best night of everyone, right, honey?" my mom said, touching my dad's shoulder.

"Yeah, now go to sleep, Carmen. You have school to-morrow," my dad said firmly.

"Yes, sir," I responded as I leaned back and tried to get comfortable.

I still wasn't that sleepy. I needed help. When my dad started talking to my mom about his week of training new staff people, that helped to tire me out. Last thing I heard him say was that he hoped Snake worked out as an assistant strength coach. My mom encouraged him to mentor the tough guy. My father said that was a good idea, but he was concerned.

I was happy to hear he was giving our friend a job. Snake had a rough life. I'll never forget the day he scared Clay, Cassie, and me when we took a shortcut through the woods. Snake taught us a good lesson. He said we have to make the most out of every opportunity life brings us, because chances don't come often. He'd been looking for a job for a while. Looked like my dad had helped him find one.

My mom told my dad that things would be fine and then kissed my dad on the cheek. It was good to see those moments. Then I closed my eyes, thanking God for my family and the wonderful day.

✪

When I was in the lunch line, I noticed everyone was laughing but me. It was Wednesday and being alone was getting rather old. However, I had no idea what I should do. Somehow I had to find a way, because I was getting tired of hanging out by myself.

Though I wanted friends, I didn't know how to approach things with Riana and Layah. We hadn't talked in a while. They weren't trying to speak to me, so I was acting like I didn't care to talk to them either.

Spence, on the other hand, was a whole different issue. Everyone knew I wanted him to forgive me. The mean looks were killing me. When I saw him eating alone once, instead of sitting by myself, I took my tray and sat in front of him. He didn't look up or anything. I wanted to get up and walk away, but I got the nerve to stay.

Finally I said, "Do you mind if I sit here?"

"If you're already sitting there, then why did you ask me?" he said coldly without looking up. "Plus, when I tell you something you can't keep it to yourself."

"Can I just apologize?"

"Do you think that an apology is going to make it all better? All my friends are laughing at me. I don't appreciate it and your little apology ain't gonna do nothin' for me."

I left my tray, ran to the bathroom, and cried. Spence wasn't all that. I did like him but not anymore because he was mean.

The bathroom door opened and I ran into a stall. I didn't want anyone to see me crying over a boy. I wasn't crying because he didn't like me; I was crying because he hurt my feelings. I saw four feet standing outside my bathroom stall.

"Carmen, we know you are in there," Riana said sweetly.

"Open up, come out of there, and talk to us," Layah said when I didn't respond.

Layah started banging on the door as if it were a punching bag. I didn't want to talk to them. No matter how much they wanted to talk to me or how much I needed to unload to them, I wasn't going to give in. They stood there for another three or four minutes before I saw the four feet walk away.

"If you wanna stay to yourself, then fine," Layah said.

"Why are we leaving? She needs to talk to us. Can't you see that she's upset?" Riana defended.

Layah said angrily, "She hears us talking about her now. If she doesn't want our help, then let her suffer."

They left. When I knew the coast was clear I came out of the bathroom. When I looked in the mirror I saw my red puffy eyes. I could hardly see them because my glasses were so fogged. I needed to clean them. Now, not only had Spence hurt my feelings, but my two ex-friends had too.

Later that day, I closed myself up in my room. My brother didn't bother me, but my sister tried to talk to me. I kept telling her to leave me alone, but she kept coming back around.

"Mom told me to ask you to fix me a snack," she begged from the other side of my closed door.

My mother was downstairs in the basement painting, and she had put Clay in charge, but it seemed as if I was always the one who had to fix the snacks. I didn't feel like getting out of my bed. Cassie wanted to be a big girl. This was her chance.

"You're nine now. It is time for you to fix your own snack," I said.

"Why are you being so mean? Are you mad at me?" Cassie asked.

Getting up and opening my door I said, "I'm not mad at you. I am just frustrated. Can you understand that?"

"That's all you had to say," Cassie said as she walked away from the door with pride. "I am old enough to fix my own snack. Hope you feel better."

I leaned against the wall in the hall and realized I shouldn't have been so mean to her. My sister was cool. I went into the kitchen to help. I fixed her a peanut-butter-and-jelly sandwich. While I was at it, I went ahead and fixed Clay and my mom one too. I went into Clay's room first, thinking he would bite my head off.

To my surprise he said, "Hey, Sis! What's up?"

"You're actin' nice," I said, glad I hooked him up with a bite. "Here, I made this for you."

"Tight, Carmen, thanks. You know I love P&J."

I laughed. "Well, don't get too happy. I poured your milk, but I couldn't fit it on the tray. Your glass is on the kitchen table."

He dashed by me and headed into the kitchen. My brother was silly. I was happy to see he wasn't sweating the adoption stuff.

Next I walked to take the tray to my mom. She saw me and said, "Thanks, honey, sit it there. How was your day?"

I hesitated. *Do I tell her the truth?* She and I hadn't talked much about boys before, but I wanted to talk about them. However, I was a little nervous.

Putting her paintbrush down, she said, "Carmen, talk to me. What's on your mind?"

"Can I ask you a deep question?" I said, walking back over to her.

"Sure, what is it?"

"It's boys. I don't understand them."

She cleared her throat, smiling at the subject. "Are you saying you like boys now?"

"No, ma'am. I'm just trying to understand them. Can you explain them, please?"

She held out her hand and we sat on the couch in her office. "What do you want to know?"

"There is this boy Spence in my class. and he told me that he missed seeing me on weekends. He told me not to say anything, but I told my friends. . . ."

"Oh, are you talking about the president of Virginia State's grandson?"

I went on to tell her the whole thing. That he was who she thought he was, what I'd told my friends, and how I felt about being isolated. She was great to talk to because she just listened.

"You two were nice to each other at the football

games. Well . . . it's not right to betray anyone's confidence," she said, brushing my hair back behind my ear.

"I know. Now he won't even talk to me. I tried to apologize, Mom, but he wouldn't listen either. Are all boys this stubborn?"

"Not just boys can be stubborn, but girls can be sometimes as well. I don't like this business about you not speaking to your friends. Everybody makes mistakes," she said as I looked perplexed. "Let me put it like this: How would you feel if you told someone a secret and they blabbed. Just treat people like you want to be treated. Remember to pray about all this."

"Thanks for the chat, Mom. Hope you like the sandwich."

"I will. This was sweet of you," she said before biting into it. "We're going to Bible study tonight."

"Bible study," I whined. "I don't want to go."

"Too bad," she said, not giving in to my pity party. "You're going."

⭐

Later, as I sat in the church, I found it very interesting that the Bible lesson was "Do unto others as you would have them do unto you." I was in the room with my peers. Mr. Meadows, our teacher, asked us what that meant to us. Struggling with that area, I did not want to answer.

However, when I was called upon, I thought carefully

about what I did think that meant and said, "Don't do something to someone that you wouldn't want done to you."

"Would you like to elaborate on that?" Mr. Meadows asked me.

Before I could speak, a lump came into my throat. I thought about what my mom had said earlier. Just like I had told Layah and Riana not to tell, Spence had told me not to tell, but I did. And just like I wanted forgiveness from Spence, Riana and Layah wanted forgiveness from me.

Out of my mouth I confessed, "This is weird because I understand this a little too much now. I have not been the best friend to my buddies, Riana and Layah. They had done something to me and I refused to forgive them. But I wanted forgiveness from someone else, and I wasn't willing to give it myself. Sometimes it is just so hard to do things right."

"That's a good lesson that you learned. I'm glad you got it now," Mr. Meadows said.

"Me too. I didn't even want to come."

"That's how good God is, Carmen Browne. He gives us what we need when we don't even know we need it."

❂

For the past several days in school, I had been trying to seek Spence out in school. On this day, I had a different mission. I was looking for Riana on the bus.

"Can I sit next to you?" I asked as I saw Riana sitting by herself.

"Sure," she said as she slid over.

"I just wanted to tell you what a jerk I have been."

It was so easy apologizing to Riana. She just listened and forgave me.

"You're so nice, Riana. You're not supposed to forgive me."

"Why shouldn't I? Sometimes I need forgiveness too. If you would have talked to me, you could have seen that what you were mad at Layah and me for, you didn't have to be."

"What do you mean?"

"Hunter overheard us talking in music."

"You guys never told?" I said, stunned.

"No, Hunter told everyone a bunch of stuff. I guess I owe you an apology because I stopped caring about telling you the truth."

We hugged.

Getting Layah to forgive me was a totally different ball game. She made me suffer for the whole day before she finally let me off the hook.

"I forgave you this morning," she told me at the end of the day. "I just wanted to make you sweat it out like you did us. But that's cool. You're my girl. My dad's having company over tomorrow, and my cool grandma is here for a week. Maybe you all can spend the night with me?"

"I'll ask my mom," I said, so happy to be invited.

"Yeah, me too," Riana chimed in.

Being with them, I wondered how could I have ever doubted them? We went together better than a peanut-butter-and-jelly sandwich. We vowed to always talk through stuff before accusing each other of things. Spence might stay mad at me forever, but it didn't matter anymore. Now I had my best friends back. Thankfully, Riana, Layah, and I were in perfect harmony.

4

Deaf Ear

Miss Pryor had become my favorite teacher ever. She listened to me and she helped me overcome every problem I brought to her. Actually she was my first African-American teacher ever, and I really loved that too. She was so down. All of the class thought she was tight. However, when she gave us another report to do, we all grumbled.

"Another paper," I blurted out with frustration after half my class also whined about the same thing.

Riana leaned over to me, rolled her eyes, and said, "Oh, come on, Carmen, I don't know why you are complaining about it.

You got a hundred . . . the best grade in the class on the last paper. It was like an easy A for you."

I gave her a crazy look, because writing my paper on affirmative action was not simple at all. Just because I got a good grade on the other one, now the expectations would be so high—not only from the teacher but from my parents too.

"Another paper, Layah," I said loudly as I tried to talk over other kids also unhappy with the assignment.

"Calm down, everyone," my teacher said with authority, hushing up all the side chatter. "You all haven't even let me tell you what the topic is. I just hear side conversations. Most of you are speaking negatively, saying you can't write a paper. Class, let me speak your language. I'm not hearing that."

Miss Pryor went on to say that to succeed in life we couldn't be lazy. She believed in each of us, and we sat and listened to her tell us *can't* was a word not allowed in her classroom.

She scolded, "You guys are in fifth grade, soon to be in middle school next year. There are no shortcuts; your minds need to be challenged."

I heard her, but I still didn't want to write another paper. Deep down, it wasn't my parents or my teacher that I didn't want to let down. I didn't want to disappoint me. So I gave an ugly look, showing that I wasn't sure I could do it.

"And, Carmen Browne, no long face from you either. I see you back there." I slid down in my seat some. "No, you sit up," she said, calling me out. "We were all moved by that wonderful paper you wrote about affirmative action. Taking a stand and pointing out that until all the biases in people could be erased, we need barriers in place was very insightful.

"You said it in your own words, and it moved us. You challenged us to really take personal opinions to heart. And, class, that's what a paper is supposed to do. I know each of you can embrace your feelings, put it into well-thought-out words, and make us feel your position."

All the bad postures, long faces, and uninterested looks went away. We started sitting up in our seats, leaning forward, and actually listening to Miss Pryor. She cared about us so much that she wanted to pull us beyond our comfort zone.

"I'm going to push you. So lose that bad, negative attitude. Leave it behind because I'm tightening up. My goal is to get you all ready for the next level. Every student out of my class is going to be ready. One thing I've always tried to teach you all is that you must approach your assignments expecting to do well. So, are you all ready to write a paper?"

"Yes, Miss Pryor," we said in unison, still unsure.

"Last semester, I gave you guys a topic, and I wanted you to choose whether you were for or against it. This time, I want to you to choose the subject. I have a general statement that will apply to whatever you choose," she told us.

At first I liked the idea of choosing what I'd write on. Though I did great on the last paper, I had a hard time researching and fully understanding the subject of affirmative action. However, at least then I knew exactly what to write about.

Oh, my gosh, how will I choose a topic? I said to myself in a panicked way.

She wrote on the blackboard, *I would change the world by . . .* I was so bummed out because nothing came to mind. As everyone wrote it down, I was really feeling my paper was gonna be horrible. Shaking my head, I had to think positive. Somehow, someway, God would lead me to a way I'd want to change the world. I had to not be negative and believe.

"Also, guys, we'll make it fun and do a contest again. I'll choose the top three papers. The winners will get five homework passes, and your papers will be on display in the front school window," our teacher said to motivate us even more.

Riana was so excited. "Passes for no homework, yeah! Okay, I know what I'm going to write about, yeah. You want to know?"

I couldn't look at her. I was jealous. However, I'd just learned that friends gotta be happy for each other.

So without a topic of my own, I said, "Tell me, girlfriend."

"I want to be a marriage counselor when I grow up. I can help both sides face the true bad points about themselves. See, if I am one, I can help married people stay together like my aunt and her husband," Riana voiced, motioning for me to approve.

Truly impressed, I uttered, "Wow, that's a great way to change the world."

She asked me if I knew what I wanted to write about. I told her no. She was so cool, telling me not to worry. My dear buddy told me I'd have something soon.

When we went out to recess that day, everybody was talking about what they were going to write about—except me. I had no clue. The paper wasn't due for two months, but I was already behind most of the class. I didn't know how to change the world.

✪

"My teacher gave us a hard thing to do," I said in a baby voice to my parents later that evening as we sat around the dinner table.

"Come on, Carmen, with your bright ideas," my dad said as he wiped the sauce from my chin with a napkin. "You're always coming up with ways to make this world a better place. You'll have no problems finding the right answer to that paper. You know I expect another A, don't you?"

"Charles, don't put pressure on that baby," my mom said to him.

"Yeah, Dad," I just sorta said without thinking.

My mom smiled at me. It was fun being on her side to gang up on my dad in a joking way. He took the clean side of his napkin and softly swung it at me.

My brother and sister were both trying to hurry because they needed to finish their homework. Clay hadn't started, but Cassie had been at it since she first got home from school, and she still wasn't done. Third grade was hard for her. I tried to tell her that at the beginning of school, but she thought it was going to be so easy. It might not have been hard for her in the first semester, but now even she had a big project due in social studies. Cassie had to construct an island, with seas and mountains and plateaus and stuff. Maybe I shouldn't be complaining about my paper. It could be harder.

Clay was awfully quiet and looked gloomy as he played with his mac and cheese. My parents didn't ask him what was going on. I knew that they had been talking to him, though. And I figured he would tell me if he wanted me to know, but for now I just inwardly prayed he would cheer up. *Yeah, maybe that was it,* I thought, as if a light bulb was going off in my mind. *I can make the whole world happy. That's a dumb thought. How would I make the whole world happy? I still don't have a topic to write about. Oh, come on, Carmen, think, think.*

The next day, I still had no topic. But when we were in music class and Ms. Hastings told us about the upcoming talent show that the PTA was putting on, I had another focus. When our music teacher encouraged all of us to enter, tons of ideas for performing came through my brain. I could sing a cappella. Or I could sing while my sister played the guitar, which she was sorta good at. Or I could try to convince my friends to be in a group with me.

That last idea was sounding really great since it was Friday night and we were headed to Layah's for a sleepover. I couldn't wait to spend time with my friends. My mom couldn't drop me off soon enough. Before she left, though, she saw where I'd be staying and met Layah's grandma. Her dad came up and said hi before heading out for a dinner date.

We were having a blast with her grandma. She was from Mississippi. I'd never met anyone from there before. Her Southern accent was cute.

In the middle of the family room was a grand piano. Her grandma headed over to it and sat on the bench after we ate her yummy fried chicken. We all followed her.

"Can y'all sang?" she asked as she struck a chord.

Layah sat down and started singing "Amen" to the melody. Riana followed and I slid right in the middle with a cool, soft soprano. We sounded so good. Layah's grandma even said so. I wanted to be in a group with them. We could be like Pure Grace. I would have to ask them about it. How could they turn me down when our friendship was back on track and we could flow like that with our voices?

Later that night after watching a Disney movie, my

girlfriends agreed that they were tired of TV. I knew I wanted to talk about the group thing, but I didn't know how to do it. Layah's grandma came by and said good night. When she shut the door, we still needed something to do. I hoped they'd be open to my idea.

"And what are we going to do now?" Riana asked in a bored tone.

"Let's talk about the talent show," I said with wide eyes brighter than the sun.

Riana said, "But you're the one who wants to sing in the talent show."

I was really into the idea at school. However, now I wanted the three of us to do it. I had to convince them. However, after they listened to me go on and on about why us being in a group would be a great idea, they gave me crazy looks.

"Girl, please, why don't you just do it? You don't need us to be up there with you. You have the best voice any-way. A girls' group?" Layah questioned as she pretended to be joking. "Uh-uh. I'm tuned out to that bad idea."

"Okay, how 'bout this? We don't have to talk about being in the talent show or really being a real group. Can't we sing something to God?" I asked when they didn't seem to be excited about anything that I was saying. "Maybe we could just sing and just see how we sound. Please, you all."

They finally agreed. I guess because I was getting on their nerves so bad. And when I hit a note, hoping that they would blend in with me, the chord we struck had to be the worst note in history.

"You're not even trying," I said, folding my arms and pouting a little.

Layah suggested, "I just don't want to sing a note that's so boring. Let's sing a song."

"Okay, what gospel songs do you all know?" I asked, trying to be flexible.

They named off some songs I didn't know. I named off some songs neither of them knew. It was looking like my idea was a bad one.

Trying to stay positive, I just blurted out, "What about 'Amazing Grace'?"

When they both agreed, it was on. We determined who'd sing what note, and then we struck out making worse noise then when we sang just the ugly note.

"You guys make me sick," I said in a mean tone before leaving out of Layah's room and unintentionally slamming the door.

I just sat in Layah's family room alone. I was secretly hoping that my two friends would come see me sad and agree to do it right or at least really, really try so we could even see if there was something there. They never came to the family room. Her grandmother did, though. She sat in the chair across from me as if she was my grandma, taking interest in the fact that I wasn't happy. I hated that I was sad, but I couldn't help it.

She mirrored my posture and asked, "So what's going on with Ms. Carmen?"

I didn't want to burden an older person with my drama, but on the other hand I wanted to get out what was bothering me so bad.

"Well, I wanted my friends to try and sing with me. See, even our music teacher says that the three of us have the best voices in the whole class. There's this talent show, and I wanted us to sing in it, but they don't want to. So I compromised and said, 'Okay, let's just sing for the fun of it.' They agreed, but the way they were singing—they weren't even trying. Then when I left, I heard them laughing through the door. They don't even care that they hurt my feelings. I might as well just go home." I started to cry.

"I'm sure you're thinking, with friends like that, who needs enemies?"

I looked up at her and slowly nodded my head. I wiped my face. Then I leaned back on the couch and wallowed some more.

"Layah told me that the last couple of months, you girls have been mad at each other and made up more times than I can even keep up with. I'm sure there were even some more riffs between you all that you don't remember.

"Layah and I talk a lot. Though I'm certain she hasn't told me everything, she's told me more than a bunch of times that you all got into it. But you guys have always gotten back together."

This time is different, I thought to myself. *How could my friends not really, really try my idea?* Boy, was I mad at them.

"If your friends don't want to be a group, then you have to be okay with that. Remember, you care about how they feel too. You like them for who they are, not because you want to be or do something that they won't do. Am I making sense now?"

I hated to admit it, but her grandma was right. I nodded my head. She smiled.

"And Layah does take some of your suggestions. I'm so happy you and Riana have persuaded her into wanting to dress more like a girl than the tomboy stuff she used to wear. You're a good influence, Carmen, but I see you're strong-willed. She's stubborn. The two of you have to give and take to be friends. No one person can always have it their way all the time.

"So you shouldn't assume your friends know you're hurt. Be honest and really tell them why you feel the way you do. Don't tell them you all sound good when you all know it might take work," she said, looking at me in a puzzled way, hoping that I got at least some of what she said.

Curling the corners of my mouth upward, I showed her grandma that I got it. I really appreciated her taking time out to give me those hints. I got up and gave her a hug.

Then I walked back into Layah's room, apologized for

slamming the door, and said, "Okay, if you guys don't want to sing in this group, then I will be disappointed, but I'll understand. I really love you guys and I'm really excited that we have singing in common. And, yeah, Riana, you sing really soft but very sweet. And, Layah, girl, you wish you had a soprano voice, but your alto voice is so cool. Everybody else likes it but you. I just know if the three of us come together and just let our friendship show through our voices. . . ."

"You can stop now," Layah said as she cut me off. "Riana and I thought about it and talked about it while you weren't in here. We agreed that if you walked back in here and apologized for slamming the door, we'd try to sing the right way."

I hugged both of them so tight, and the next note that we sang—though it didn't sound great—certainly sounded better. We had potential and we agreed to keep practicing. Who could ask for more? Layah's grandma was right. When we want our friends to see things our way, we have to tell the truth. We have to speak from the heart, and then leave it to whatever they give back. In this case it worked out, but I really learned a lesson. And as long as my girls are going to try, what more can I ask for?

✪

Layah, her dad, and grandma dropped me off the next day. I was so happy; Riana, Layah and I were tight. The smile left my face when my annoying sister met me at the door.

She said, "You don't want to go downstairs. Clay and Dad are going at it again."

"Stop exaggerating," I told her as I put my hand in her face and slightly moved her back so I could get in the door.

"Quit pushing me. I'm going to tell Mom," she said. I shrugged my shoulders, showing her I didn't care. "Stop being so mean to me, Carmen. I'm trying to tell you what's going on downstairs."

When I started going up, my sister just sat down on the stairs, defeated. Then I remembered me wanting my friends to sing in my group. That wasn't what they wanted to do, but when I spoke from the heart they came around.

So I went back down the stairs sat down beside Cassie and said, "Sorry for not hearing you out. Talk to me. What's going on? You told me not to go downstairs, but I know that's because you really want me to go. So why are you playing?"

"Okay, I'll tell you. Clay has just been really mean and Dad's been yelling at him. And Mom's been yelling at Dad, and she's been yelling at me. It's been so bad. I didn't hear everything, but I know Clay talks to you more, and I just wish that you'd care about our family more than your new friends. You're always talking to them on the phone, you're always at a slumber party with them, and you even do homework with them sometimes. You're never my big sister anymore."

"Okay, I'll try and do better," I said, feeling bad that I'd hurt her.

Cassie could be making more out of stuff than was there. However, to be on the safe side, I decided to check downstairs for myself.

"So will you try to help Clay now? He is making Mom really sad, talking about going and finding his other parents. Come on," she said, pulling my arm as I sat my bag down by the door and walked downstairs.

As soon as I went down a couple of stairs, Cassie went behind me and sorta pushed me along. Before I could get to the last stair I heard my dad yell out, "Listen, no more talk about finding any family. Your mom and I already told you, we'd look at that when you're a little older. Right now we know what's best, and you don't need to get into any of that mess."

"Mess! You trying to say my real parents are a mess; that's for me to judge, Dad," Clay said back loudly.

"Boy, you have absolutely no respect for authority. I'm getting sick and tired . . ." I could see my mom pulling my dad away from Clay.

"Honey, honey, just calm down," my mom said in an upset voice.

"I do respect authority," my brother said, not letting it go. "I've heard what y'all told me, but that doesn't mean that what I want inside is going to go away, you know. I just wish you would respect my feelings."

"Well, Son, if respecting your feelings means letting

you go down a road that won't lead you to where you think it will, we're not letting that happen."

Clay said in a teary voice, "I guess I'm just stuck here then."

The next thing I knew, Clay flew by Cassie and me. My mom burst into tears and my dad hugged her. Cassie rushed up to her side.

"Mommy, don't cry," Cassie said as she hugged the back of my mom's waist.

Dad looked up at me and said, "You guys shouldn't be listening in on people's conversations."

"Dad, I was just coming down . . ." I tried to explain so he wouldn't be mad.

He voiced in an upset tone, "I don't want to hear it, Carmen. Don't do that again."

"Sweetie, go and check on your brother," my mom looked up at me and said nicely. Before I went upstairs, I heard her say to my dad, "I'm losing my son. Why doesn't he know that I'm his mom? Why can't that be enough?"

I knocked on my brother's door and opened it up at the same time. He was stretched out across his bed with his head buried in his pillow. "I care about how you feel, Clay," I said. I didn't say anything else; I waited for him to respond.

There was silence for a while. I couldn't leave, though. So I stood there.

Finally, he got up and came over to me with his watery eyes and said, "All right, if you care about my feelings, then you've got to help me, Carmen. You've got to promise me you'll help me find my other parents, without Mom and Dad knowing. Or should I say without *your* mom and dad's permission? Can you do that? Can you help me?"

No was the answer in my heart to that question. However, knowing that was the last thing I wanted to do but the only thing I could do to let him know that I was in his corner, I had to agree.

"Carmen, I knew you would come around for me. We're going to find my parents. Thanks so much, cuz we can do this without Mom and Dad, because on this subject they've got a deaf ear."

5

Loud Noise

Mom, " I said, screaming through the house when I got home from school. "I got a carnation today. Spencer gave me a carnation. Oh, my gosh, Mom, look."

"It's so pretty. A peppermint carnation," she said closely, looking at the white flower sprinkled with a little red. "Very, very lovely. And what does the card say?"

I could tell the way she asked that she wasn't really sure how she felt about me getting a flower from a boy. Actually, I wasn't sure either. I thought Spence would never talk to me again, and even if he did, I wasn't sure if I'd want to talk back to him after the way he'd treated me. But all my doubts about never being his friend again went out the window when he walked by my desk and gave me a sweet-smelling flower.

"Mom, I was so surprised. And in a good way, Mom. Ya know?" I talked rather loud with excitement.

"Well, tell me what the card says, please, ma'am."

I couldn't even read it again. I was so giddy. I got a card and flower from Spencer. I handed her the envelope and she read the pink note inside that my classmate wrote.

> Carmen,
> Sorry I was such a jerk. I shouldn't have been so mean. Can we be friends again? Hope so.
> Spencer

My mom nodded her head firmly once. "Very nice note. Good to see the young man can apologize for being wrong. You know your dad always gives me flowers and special little gifts just because. In this day and age it's nice to see a young boy acting like a gentleman. And as pumped as you are about this, I'm sure you told him you'd be his buddy again."

Smiles would just not leave my face. I then hugged her. I was happy that she was happy for me. Boy, it was great the way I could talk to her. My dad wouldn't at all like that I was so excited about getting a flower from a boy, even though he does those things for my mom. And even though Spencer had hurt my feelings by not talking to me for weeks, I had decided to forget him even before he said he was sorry. But now, this way was even better.

I wasn't the only one who got a flower in our class. Riana got one from Hunter, and hers was pink. Her card only said, "From Hunter." But you would have thought it had a hundred of the nicest words on it, the way that Riana was smiling so. Actually, she and I both were really happy. Layah thought we were crazy. Actually, I realized that maybe boys weren't so weird after all.

My dad came home with four bouquets of roses. One was yellow for Cassie. Two batches were red for my mom, and then he gave me a pink set. They were so pretty. He told me I'd always be his special Valentine. Boy, did I love my dad.

After I did my homework that cold afternoon, I sat at my desk and stared at all the flowers I'd gotten that day. My mom helped me place them in one of her glass vases. The carnation looked lovely nestled in there with the roses.

Quickly, I turned around when I heard my bedroom door slam and saw Clay looking mean. "Carmen, get out of the daydream. Aren't you supposed to be helping me find my other family?"

I couldn't even answer him truthfully. Though I'd told him I would help, I'd been avoiding him and that task. He'd caught me doing nothing. Oh, boy!

"Come with me to look on the computer and see if there is something telling me how I can find my family.

Are you going to help? You know what, Carmen? Don't help. I'll do this alone and then tell ya once I'm outta here."

I stood up and went over to my brother before he could head out of my room. Placing my hands on his shoulders I said, "Look, I'm in this with you. Cut me some slack. I'll help for real, okay? I didn't even know you were home. And to be honest, Clay, I was hoping that you would change your mind."

"No way!" Clay yelled out. "I told you I wanted to do this and you said you would help me. If you are turning back on your word, then just tell me. I really don't have time. . . ." He mumbled some of the rest.

Clay was acting like a baby. He was trying to act all tough with his arms folded. I told him I'd help, but I wasn't gonna beg him not to be mad at me. One thing I learned from the time Spencer got mad at me was that I can't always make people come around. Sometimes they need their space.

"Fine, then," I bluffed and told him as I moved to head back to my desk.

He gently reached for my sweater, tugged me back, and said, "Wait, I do need your help. I just want to find them. Sorry I was edgy."

I told him it was cool and then we walked downstairs. We peeked around the corner to make sure my mom wasn't near the computer. She was in the next room working on artwork. I asked her if it was okay if I went online and had Clay help me with research. She said sure. I know she thought the research I meant was my paper. Not telling the whole truth made me feel bad.

Though Clay was computer savvy, I guess he didn't want to look for his other family on his own. I still felt dishonest to our parents. Dad had told him to drop the idea, and here I was helping him. Not good.

"Glad we're working together. This is the best time. Mom thinks I'm helping you. We can find some numbers, make some calls, and who knows? In a second I might have my answer," my brother said as we headed into the computer room.

I didn't wanna bust his bubble, but it was already the end of the day. I was sure most companies would be closing at five o'clock. However, I kept my negative thoughts to myself and tried to make the best of the time we had.

After Clay ran the search for adoption agencies, we had 1,232 sites that came up. He dropped his head in despair then. I told my brother not to be down. I asked him to go back and put in Virginia adoption agencies, and when he did that it narrowed it down a lot. Now we only had 56 to check out. Problem was, it was now four forty-five.

We didn't have time to call anybody, I thought, but Clay found the two in Charlottesville. That was the city from which we'd moved. He dialed the first number in that town and bit his nails as the line connected.

"It's busy," he said as he pounded his wrist on the table.

"It's okay. It might not be easy, but we are going to find out the info that you want. Try this one," I told him as I pointed to the other number on the screen he'd highlighted.

My brother didn't even try. He got up and exited out of the room. He was so bummed out. I hated that this was getting to him. I followed him to his room.

Standing just inside his doorway, I said, "Don't give up; we are going to find your parents."

"Find his parents," I heard the nagging voice say loudly.

Clay's eyes got really big. I turned around. I could have passed out right there. Boy, did I wish I could take back those words. It was Cassie being nosy, and I had given her more information than she needed.

"Oooh, I'm going to tell. You guys are trying to find his other parents. Mama and Daddy told him not to do that. Oooh."

Quickly, as my sister got louder, I went over and covered her mouth with my left hand. I was so mad at her. I pulled her out of the room. I let her look into my eyes and they said, *help me out here.*

I looked back into her eyes and asked, "What can I do to keep you quiet?"

Slowly, when I let go of her mouth, she said, "Chores, lots and lots of chores. I'll let you do my chores and I won't say anything."

"I have not told them anything that is not true," I tried to defend.

"Yeah, but you are doing something that they told you not to do. You're not telling the truth about what's going on, and that's telling a lie. Because you'll be doing my work around here, I won't tell," she said as she winked at me.

She was such a pest, but I couldn't deny her words. I stepped back into my brother's room. I didn't even know whether to tell him that Cassie really knew what we were doing or not. Oh, it was such a mess.

"Don't even ask," I finally blurted out to him so I wouldn't have to tell him one way or the other. "We're cool. We'll get back on this tomorrow."

Sliding back out his door, I thought about what Cassie had said. My sister was right. Leaving out important information was the same as lying, particularly when the information left out would be bad if my parents knew it. *Lord, help me figure this whole thing out,* I thought.

★

"Are you sure we can pull this plan off?" I asked rather loudly while Layah's dad pumped gas before taking the three of us to the mall.

"Shhh," my feisty friend uttered. "My dad's right there and he can read your lips through the glass. We went over and over and over this plan. Why does it seem like the two of you guys are wimping out on me?"

"'Cause, Layah, we're not as tough as you," Riana said in a mousy-toned voice as she looked out the window and saw the pretty snowfall.

Layah was right about one thing; we had gone over and over and over the plan. Her dad had picked Riana and me up, and we were heading to the mall to meet Riana's mom, or so Mr. Golf thought. But, in reality, we weren't going to meet any parents. The three of us were just going to hang out at the mall alone, proving to our parents once and for all that we were grown-up and that they could trust us.

Then when we were ready to go, our plan was that we were going to call Riana's mom and ask her to come and get us. We planned to stand in front of the movie theater. Riana's mom would think Mr. Golf wanted to go see a movie. Since Mr. Golf was planning to go see one as soon as he dropped us off, we figured we weren't really lying to our folks; we were just sorta stretching the facts here and there. We felt this was a fail-proof idea. And I went ahead with the plan because it was all for a good cause—to prove a point that we could handle the independence.

"Don't y'all crack on me," Layah said as she hugged the two of us in a bear embrace.

"Ugh, that hurts," Riana said when Layah wouldn't let go of either of us.

"Yeah, come on, that hurts," I said.

She finally let go and said, "Okay, I'm toughening you guys up."

"You're toughening them up?" her father asked, star-
tling us when he got into the car. "Why do they need to
be tougher?"

"Oh, it's just girl talk, Dad," Layah answered back,
smiling at Riana and me because she dodged a close one.

"Are you sure your mom's at the mall, Riana?" Layah's
dad questioned as we saw snow falling.

My friend's eyes got wide. Layah tugged on her long
hair, motioning for her to answer. Riana squirmed, not
wanting to have to tell Layah's dad something that wasn't
true.

"Maybe I should park and walk in with you guys," Mr.
Golf said as he pulled into the mall.

Riana piped up and said, "No, my mom said that
she'd see us right inside. Plus, sir, your movie should be
starting soon. You don't want to miss the beginning."

"Actually, I need to work on a case. I think I'm going
to skip the movie and head on back to the house. I won't
take off until I know you're safe inside. Layah, wave at me
when you all are with Mrs. Anderson," he said.

I was the last one out of the car and I slammed the car
door. "You're going to break my dad's car," Layah said to
me.

Feeling bad I said, "I'm sorry. I guess I'm just
nervous."

"Oh, come on, this is going to be great," Layah said as
we headed to the door.

Riana went in first, and then Layah walked through

79

the heavy doors. I stared at Mr. Golf, unable to follow through with our crazy idea. Shivering in the cold, he rolled down his window and told me to head inside. I nodded and went that way.

Before I got to open it, Layah came charging out. She ran over to her dad's car and told him something. She stepped back and waved bye to her father.

As her dad pulled away I pitifully watched, hoping he would come back and pick us up. Layah saw I was still having trouble with it all, and she grabbed my hand and pulled me inside. "Come on before my dad sees you're still out here. He'll turn around, girl, he will. Let's go."

"What are we going to do anyway?" I asked, now thinking this was a bad idea.

"The same thing we always do when our parents are in the mall with us . . . browse and make a list of stuff we want to buy."

I was the only hesitant one at that moment and my feet just didn't seem to follow the two of them. What had I done? I so hoped nothing went wrong. Layah turned back and yelled for me to come on. It was like the brakes were released and I caught up with the two of them.

I certainly didn't want them to leave me behind. An hour later all my inhibitions were gone. Layah, Riana, and I were having such a good time going from store to store, picking out all the things we would buy if we had some money.

Tired of dreaming of what I wanted to buy, I particularly liked it when we all went into Claire's. It's the best accessory store in the world. We each had twenty dollars spending money and were ready to buy two gifts for each other under the five-dollar price mark and food for lunch. I got a cool sports watch for Layah and an adorable earring holder for Riana.

Next, we went to the food court. It was so exciting to be able to choose whatever I wanted without hearing my mom say "nope, can't get that" or, "nope, not that." I was grown and I loved it. I could totally handle it. We made the right call doing this, I felt. I finally admitted that to both of my girlfriends as we dove into the pizza we went in together to purchase.

When I got up to go buy a blizzard from Dairy Queen, I asked if they wanted one also and said I'd treat. When they said yes, I reached down for my purse. I didn't see it. Frantically, I yelled for my friends to help. We all looked around for my pocketbook but couldn't find it.

All of a sudden, Snake walked up to us and said, "Is this what you are looking for, little Browne?"

"Oh, my gosh. Who is that?" Riana said, clutching my arm.

"That's Snake. He's cool, real cool. He works for my dad," I answered before looking at him. "How'd you get my purse?"

"I took it back from a guy who took it off the back of your chair a second ago. You've got to watch your stuff," Snake said as he handed it to me.

"Wow, thanks. These are my two girlfriends," I said. "Layah and Riana, this is Snake."

"What's up, y'all?" he said as my friends waved at him. "Little Browne, where's your parents? What's up? Where's your brother, sister, somebody? I know you ain't just out here with your girls chilling in the mall like you're grown and all. Shoot, you can't even hold on to your purse."

I badly tried explaining, "No, we're not alone. Our folks are . . ."

The three of us started going back and forth telling different stories. None of them made sense, added up, or was believed by Snake.

"I'll see you later, Snake," I said when my friends just pulled me away from him.

I was sick and tired of getting yanked all day long, but that time I was happy they saved me because with Snake working with my dad at Virginia State, the last thing that I needed was for him to squeal on us.

I loved this new mall. The coast was clear for us to shop till we dropped.

We headed to play video games in the mall arcade. Layah and I were gonna wait there as Riana went to call her mom. We were all kinda tired and really ready to go home. Before she could step away, I looked outside and was shocked to see the amount of snow outside.

"Oh, my goodness," I said to both of them, seeing thick piles of white stuff everywhere. "Look at that snow. We've got to get home."

Instead of Layah and I going to play video games, we went right to the phone with Riana. I even dug into my purse to find the fifty cents for her to call. She couldn't dial fast enough for me.

"Mom," we heard her say into the receiver. . . . "Naw, we're not home. . . . Yes, we see all the snow. . . . Huh? No, yeah, okay, okay, bye."

"What?" I said to her, shaking my friend.

"My mom said that she just knew that Layah's dad would already be on his way to take us home because of the snowstorm. She said it's hard for her to even see. So she doesn't want to come and get us and wants me to ask him to bring me home now," Riana said in a dejected voice.

"Why didn't you tell her that he wasn't here?" I asked.

Riana quickly retorted, "I'm not getting into trouble. You call your mom and tell her that her Layah's dad is not here."

Once she put it like that, I understood the dilemma. I didn't want to get into trouble. So I shouldn't want her to get into trouble either. What in the world were we gonna do?

"Okay, we've just got to think," Layah said, pacing back and forth.

Yeah, she needed to think of a new plan. It was her bold attitude that had gotten us into this whole mess. But I needed to help as well. No one made me come. However, I couldn't think of a thing. Clearly, I wasn't ready to be on my own.

Layah came up to Riana and I and said, "Let's take a taxi home."

"And when a taxi pulls us up in front of the house, then what?" I asked, trying to make sure she came up with something that wouldn't get us in trouble.

Layah replied, "We'll just tell him to let us out at the corner. We'll have to get dropped off at the same house. I know we were all supposed to go back to our own houses, but with a snowstorm, guys, they'll just be glad that we're safe."

This didn't seem like a good thing at all. But it certainly was better than the alternative of calling our parents and letting them know we had lied. Oh, no, that just wasn't an option.

So, I held my two friends' hand and said, "Okay, we can do this. How much does a cab even cost? I don't have that much money."

"Well, I still have sixty dollars put aside my dad gave me for the dress I told him I wanted to buy," Layah said.

I reached into my wallet and said, "I've got twelve."

Riana said, "I've got seven. A cab can't be more than seventy-nine dollars."

We headed outside and stood next to the taxicab pickup sign. The snow was coming down really hard at that moment. Thankfully, it was only a minute or two before a cab came.

"Where to, little ladies?" the old, bald guy said to the three of us.

Layah gave her address and then said, "And, sir, we kinda want to know how much this fare is going to cost?"

"It'll be about fifty dollars. Do you all have that much?" he asked before moving an inch.

The three of us nodded our heads, and then he started up the car. He was going so slow. We were so scared because he couldn't see a thing. We had to be big girls. But how?

Tears started to well up in my eyes. "We shouldn't have done this. I should have called my mom."

"You're right," Riana agreed.

Layah wouldn't admit we shouldn't have done it, but she certainly looked like why in the world did we. None of us had to say it, but our parents were right. We weren't responsible enough to be out by ourselves. We were in a cab with a man we had never met, and though Layah had explained that she and her dad take cabs quite often, this was my first time and it wasn't cool. It was cold in the cab, not to mention cold outside; and even though the three of us were huddled together, I was still freezing.

"I don't know why these people don't have on their hazard lights. Oh, no, hold on, girls, hold on!" the driver said loudly.

He was about to run into a car, but he turned to the left to swerve and avoid it. The cab started spinning on the ice. I grabbed both my girlfriends' hands so hard and I prayed. *Lord, forgive us for what we have done. Please get us out of this mess.* Riana yelled out with horrendous cries and Layah started yelling at the taxi driver to hold the car steady. We were all a mess. The next thing I knew, everything was silenced by an extremely loud noise.

6

Dope Sound

"Are you ladies okay back there?" the cab driver asked in a groggy voice.

Just hearing some words was music to my ears. I figured if I could hear him, then that let me know I going to be okay. I'd never been more scared in my life.

"I'm alive! I'm alive," Riana shouted. "It looks like we just hit a tree."

"Y'all, we just had an accident," Layah said, more frightened than I'd ever seen her.

The three of us hugged each other so tight. We couldn't let go. We must have asked each other bunch of times if we were okay.

Layah took her wrist and wiped off the window. "Looks like we hit a tree. I wanna go home."

My tough buddy was shaken up. I was as well. Being at one of our houses would be such a good thing. But as the taxi driver started to turn on the car, all I heard was a wheel spinning. We weren't going forward. We were just stuck, sinking deeper and deeper into the ground.

Riana began to panic. "I've got to get home. What's gonna happen to us?"

"Your whining isn't going to help us get there any faster," Layah said to her in sort of a mean way.

I couldn't listen to either one of them. I needed to talk to the One who had the answers. We'd done it our way. I believed God could help me if I gave this big problem to Him.

So I prayed silently, *Heavenly Father, we did the wrong thing. We tried to be grown-ups and ignored what our parents have taught us. Now we've gotten ourselves stuck in the snow. It's so dark outside and so cold in this cab. Please help us get home soon and safely. In Jesus' name . . .*

Before I could say amen, the taxi radio called out to our driver. He picked up and explained to his head-quarters' station our dilemma. The urgency in his voice didn't sound good to me. After giving an estimated location, he was told to sit tight, and they would send a wrecker out to pull us.

"You crashed with three minors in the car!" his boss yelled so loud, it frightened us more than we were already. "Oh, this isn't good at all. What if their parents sue?"

All of a sudden, our driver turned off his CB, not

wanting to listen to any more of the screaming. Then he put his head down on the steering wheel. I could tell he felt really bad.

"I know your parents have got to be worried sick about you girls," he finally uttered in a concerned way without turning around to look at us. "They are really going to be worried now. It may take an extra hour or two for someone to come get us."

Layah huffed, crossed her arms, and uttered, "I should get out and push us. Or he should and I could steer us out of the hole. We can't sit here and do nothing. I want to go home."

My friend, Layah, was the bold one. I really loved that about her, but this time she needed to sit still. If she didn't see that, then I was gonna have to tell her.

When she opened up the car door, I pulled her back in and closed it. "Nope, girl, you're not going anywhere. We've followed you, but now look at us. So let's listen to the adults and wait for the wrecker."

I couldn't believe I had all that in me. Telling my strong girlfriend to calm down and actually have her listen made me feel good that I honestly told her how I felt. My work wasn't done, though. I heard Riana crying on the other side of me, and I needed to calm her down as well.

I turned to Riana and wiped a few tears from her eyes. "Don't cry. Layah and I are scared too, but you've got to calm down."

"You're right, Carmen, I've got to stay calm," Riana

said to me as she squeezed my hand that was wet from her tears.

I hated seeing Riana's pretty face so sad. Having Layah pouting on the other side of me wasn't cool either. I'd told one not to panic and take action, and I'd told the other to stay calm. I had to help give them something to do.

So I said, "Come on, y'all, let's . . . pray."

The bitterness from Layah and the sadness from Riana melted away like I wanted the snow on the ground to do. They both smiled at me. In silence, they bowed their heads and prayed. I didn't know how God would fix all this, but I knew with the three of us praying I didn't have to worry anymore.

Minutes later, we got a knock on our window. It startled us at first. We realized we were being saved. The three of us knew God was on His job. We all screamed. We thought it was going to take the wrecker a while to find us, but it only took minutes.

"A wrecker is coming, sir, thanks," our driver said as he rolled down his window for the strange guy standing there.

At first, I was really bummed out. It wasn't the wrecker. Just a nice concerned traveler offering help. Or what if the person wasn't nice? What if he wanted to kidnap us? All of a sudden I was frantic.

Then Layah's voice said some words that made me feel much better. "It's your friend that brought you your purse, Carmen."

Quickly I looked up. It was a very nice person at our window. Once again, I screamed with joy.

"Snake!" I yelled, sliding across Riana to get out of the cab.

It would have been great to see a wrecker, but this was way better. Snake was someone I knew. I looked up at the dark eerie sky and thanked God.

"Can you help us? It's so cold in there," I asked.

"I got ya, little Browne. I talked to your dad and told him that I thought I saw you get in a cab. He should be pulling up any minute," Snake said as he looked at me with a serious glare and then talked to our driver as the cabman got out. Snake's car had been parked near the mall entrance where we caught the cab. As he warmed up his car, he noticed us pulling off in the cab. Because of the bad weather, he was able to catch up to us and follow the cab. "Sir, I know the girls. One of their fathers is my boss. He's on his way and asked if they'd wait in the car with me. Do I need to pay you for their fare? You got somebody coming, right?"

"No, no money needed. I'm already in trouble for picking up minors. And I feel terrible about the accident. You just take them and get them in your car. I can bear not having heat. Someone will be here for me soon," the driver said in a gloomy voice.

Snake encouraged him as he opened the back door and motioned for Riana and Layah to come on out. "I'm just glad you all are okay. Accidents happen."

We said our good-byes to the cab driver. We also got our few bags. Climbing into Snake's warm car was a cool feeling.

"Your dad's coming, Carmen?" Riana asked as soon as we got in Snake's SUV.

Snake must have overheard her. "He'll be here in a bit."

Snake sat silently, tapping the steering wheel. He didn't even give us the third degree about our poor choice about going to the mall without supervision. What he did do was ask if we wanted to hear his latest song. We opened up and said yeah. Layah, Riana, and I loosened up a lot to his hip-hop, Christian rap tune. The song talked about how we had to respect authority even though we think we know better than the person telling us what we've got to do. If they are older than we are, then we've got to respect authority and leave the rest to God.

"I hear ya, Snake," I said when the song was done. "I really did learn a good lesson."

"Yeah, me too," Riana piped up. "Our folks know best. We weren't ready to hang out on our own."

"They shouldn't be the ones getting in trouble. It was all my fault," Layah said, holding her head down.

"It was all of our faults," I told her.

Snake turned toward us and said, "All three of you guys messed up. But, hey, nobody's perfect. You've just got to learn from your mistakes. And right now, I hate to say it, but you have to suffer the consequences because I know y'all parents are heated."

"What can we do to not get it so bad?" I asked him for quick advice.

"Y'all can handle it. Just don't have an attitude. Don't think you know everything; and be humble, for real. Tell 'em you won't do it again, and mean it."

"Thanks, Snake," I said, hoping my mom and dad would forgive me.

Snake saw lights behind him and got out. When he said it was my dad, my stomach dropped worse than the Free Fall ride at King's Dominion. What was he going to do to me? Tears just flowed down my face.

"No need to cry now," my dad said as he opened up Snake's car door for us to exit.

"He's mad," I tried to whisper to my friends. "This is not good."

"You're absolutely right, it's not good," my dad said as we all got into my family's car. "Move it!"

I quickly did exactly what I was told. When we got in, my angry father shut the door and then went over and talked to Snake. I told my girlfriends I believed we'd be in such hot water once we got back to my house. They agreed we were in trouble.

We drove in silence for a while. A part of me was wishing none of this was happening. This wasn't a dream, though. Our great plan turned out to be not so great after all.

My dad finally broke the silence and said, "What in

the world were you girls thinking? No, don't even try to answer that one, 'cause you all *weren't* thinking."

The three of us held hands. This was not good. I'd done bad things before but never anything this crazy.

"You all scared us. And your parents should be at our house when we get there. I'm happy you're okay, but I must say I'm so disappointed in you, Carmen Browne . . . poor judgment. We've got a lot to talk about."

"Yes, Daddy," I said, of course feeling terrible about my actions.

When we got inside my house, my father motioned for us to go downstairs.

Riana went over and hugged her mama so tight. She was still shaking from the experience. Her mom kissed her head.

Layah went over to her father and said, "Sorry, I let you down, Dad." He swatted her playfully on her arm and then gave her a bear hug with a knuckle sandwich tapping her head.

I didn't know what to say. I stood there. The blank look I saw on my mom's face made me feel worse than I already did, and I didn't think that was possible. The disappointed stare she gave me made me feel worse than a girl with the flu or with an all-F report card. I mean, I felt *bad*. I wanted to say something, but I didn't know what to say.

My dad said, "Look, girls, I know you all are sorry. I rode home with you. You know you messed up, but there are some serious things we need to talk about here."

Riana's dad chimed in. "Yeah, and getting into a taxi-cab with a complete stranger and then ending up in a car accident . . ."

Riana's mom said, "Oh, my gosh, and how about plain-out lying to us? And for what? So that you guys could go to the mall and show us how grown-up you are?"

My mom finally spoke and said, "Girls, did you prove your point? Did you make your case? Do you feel grown-up now?"

I shook my head to every question she asked. My mother and I had a great relationship. I could talk to her about anything. We were starting to talk about my feelings for boys and stuff. Why in the world didn't I come to her with my plan? I could see in her eyes that, above all, she was hurt by what I'd done.

"Carmen, you've got to tell me why, honey. You've broken my trust. Why?" my mom said before she walked over to a corner.

"It's my fault, Mrs. Browne," Layah said, coming over to stand beside me. "This was my idea."

"Your idea?" Mr. Golf asked his daughter in an upset way.

"You're dating again. You're never paying me any attention, so I wanted to do something fun with my friends."

Layah let a tear well up in her eye. Quickly she wiped it away. Her father didn't look sorry he'd made his daughter feel that way.

Mr. Golf shook his head and uttered, "Well, what a pitiful way to try and get attention. You lie and jeopardize your life because you want my attention. Well, now you've messed yourself up. We won't have fun outings for a while. You'll be on punishment. This is ridiculous, coming up with something so reckless. Before I pulled off, you came to my car and told me Mrs. Anderson was inside. Girrrl . . ."

"Sir, it's my fault," Riana stood up and said as she got on the other side of me. "I really wanted them to go through with this."

"Why?" her mother asked.

Riana continued, "Mom, you always baby me. I wanted to be more like my friends. I wanted them to help me grow up some, not be so scared to try new and different things. I'm the one that convinced Carmen to do this for my sake."

"Usually, Riana, I'd whip you," her dad said, gritting his teeth. "But you wanna be so grown-up? You won't get off punishment until you're grown."

"I'm really sorry, Dad," Riana pleaded.

"You guys don't have to do this," I looked on both sides of me and said to my friends.

I didn't know what I was going to say to all our parents to make them understand our hearts. I mean, we did have good intentions. We weren't bad. I couldn't let my friends try to take the blame for me.

I stepped in front and said, "I knew what I was doing.

I surely found out that I wasn't grown, but I thought I was. We were wrong for what we did and we feel bad. When we were in that car and it was spinning around like crazy, we were all scared. We just wanted to get back to you guys and apologize for thinking that we knew more than we actually did."

My mother still didn't turn around. She was really upset. I had to say something to let her really know how sorry I was.

Speaking from my heart, I said, "I just prayed for another chance to start at the bottom and earn your trust back again, Mom."

My mother finally turned and looked at me. Her eyes were red, but I'd said something that made her really know I cared. I walked over to her and took her hand.

I said, "We all learned a valuable lesson. We now know that God made you our parents for a good reason."

Riana said, "We know that we did wrong. From now on we are going to be friends that don't get each other in trouble."

"So we're really, really sorry," I looked at all of them and said.

My mom threw her arms around me and kissed both of my cheeks. She squeezed me so hard that I felt her love for me in a weird sort of way. It was then that I knew she'd be open to forgiving me.

She said in a sincere voice, "I love you, baby, and I, too, prayed that maybe I could communicate with you a little bit better to explain to you why my no is no and give you a little bit more freedom—that's supervised."

We were connected even closer. All these people were around and she was honest with me. I loved my mom. She showed me that she understood what I was trying to do, and she planned to help me accomplish it.

"I have an open door to you, Carmen. So don't feel like you ever have to lie to me. Good can't come out of that. Out of this whole crazy episode, I hope you guys have learned that you have parents you can talk to." She kissed my forehead and then went over and talked to the other parents.

My mom made chili and the whole house smelled good. Because the storm was getting worse, my dad just encouraged everyone to stay for a while and eat. They all agreed and my friends and I talked to our parents separately before heading upstairs to my room.

We all got punishments. My folks told me they were going to take my phone and TV-watching privileges away. None of us knew when the punishments would be over, but for now the three of us were just so happy to be safe.

In my room, I told the two of them, "We've got to pray and thank God we got out of that mess okay."

"Prayer, yeah, that sounds good to me," Riana said.

Layah held out both of her hands and we joined in a circle and she began, "Father, I think I am so tough sometimes, but thank You for sending me two friends that can stand up to me and help me see that I'm not always right."

She squeezed Riana's hand and my other friend began, "And, Lord, You know I'm the opposite. I sometimes feel so weak, weaker than a little mouse, but You've given me two friends to help me get stronger. Thank You for being there for us today. We didn't deserve a way out, but I'm so happy—happy that You sent Snake and Coach Browne to help us."

She squeezed my hand and I said, "Oh, Lord, I'm happy for two friends who love me. Keep helping me get better. I know we scared our parents today and we scared ourselves, but You were there. You helped us to see that we are not ready to be on our own. You also helped us to see what they talk about in Sunday school is more than just stuff that passes the time. You're real. It wasn't until I prayed to You and asked You to help us and called on the name of Jesus that our mess got fixed. We even got good medicine from our parents, and we thank You for that too. We know You love us. We love you back. In Jesus' name, amen."

"Amen," my two friends said together.

"Have you guys thought any more about your papers?" I asked, thinking about bringing home a good grade for my parents.

"Yeah, I told you about mine," Riana said as I sat on my bed and scratched my head.

"Oh, yeah, that's right. You're going to do the whole thing on parents not splitting up," I said.

Riana agreed, "Right, so I can change the world and

make marriage last forever. Have you thought of anything, Layah?"

"Not really, I got a good grade on the other paper. I am going to just breeze through this one," Layah said under her breath.

I couldn't believe what my friend was saying, not wanting to challenge herself. She was a competitor in every way. I knew grades were no exception to that rule.

"Come on, you're not telling the truth. I know you want a good grade," I said.

"Okay, okay, I do, but I don't know what to write about, do you?" Layah asked me.

"Yeah, Carmen, what are you writing about?" Riana also questioned.

"I don't know what I want to write about. But I do know I want to sing for the talent show." I got up from the bed and turned on a little music from my stereo that just played a beat, and I started dancing. "Come on, y'all, we've got to think of something."

After a few bad notes we started getting it together. We went back to singing "Amazing Grace," and at that point each of us thought about the words. We also thought about the day's events. How God brought us through was some real amazing grace. It sounded so mature that an audience noticed. Our parents clapped and cheered from down the hall, and they asked us to come down.

As we walked I thought, *Wow, we were lost out there*

trying to do it on our own with the car spinning out of control, and God helped us find our way home safely. With smiles on our faces, we knew we had something. They made us sing it over again and that made us feel good.

My dad joked as we saw our company to the door, "Little ladies, you all might be hardheaded, but you sisters can sure 'sang.' That was a dope sound."

7

Indoor Voice

"I'm not telling you ladies anymore. Keep it down. You're in the library," the strict librarian, Mrs. Walsh, said to Layah, Riana, and me as we tried holding in our giggles. "This is the third time I've told you all to be quiet. I'm serious. I'm not telling you anymore."

As soon as Mrs. Walsh left, the three of us really cracked up. We couldn't help it. We were so silly that day. We were supposed to be quiet, doing research for our papers, but we were just silly and it was fun.

"Wait, y'all, I've got a joke," I said to my friends in a mischievous way when they went back to doing work.

Riana said, knowing I was stalling,

"Come on, Carmen, we're going to get in trouble. You need to figure out a subject that you want to write about, and go find a book over there."

"No, no," Layah said. "Let's hear the joke."

In a loud whisper, I began telling the joke. However, if I would have known that our librarian was so serious about us being out of chances, I wouldn't have said a word. I didn't even get to tell the joke. We all knew we were in serious trouble when she headed straight for us with a mean look on her face from behind the checkout desk.

"Girls, get your stuff," she said firmly, "and follow me."

"But, Mrs. Walsh," Layah said, trying to get us a way out of it. "Y'all, she's ignoring me."

Riana looked at me in a mean way and mouthed *I told you so*. I really felt bad because I was the one who kept instigating us to talk. Deep down, I didn't want them finishing their paper because I didn't have a topic myself. I didn't want anybody to be finished. I couldn't control the rest of the class, but I certainly could keep my friends from being focused. So idle time got me into trouble and not just me, but my friends too. As we picked up our stack of books and followed Mrs. Walsh, I dropped my head, not feeling good at all.

In all my years of elementary, I had never been taken to the office. I remember when I first got to school last year, Layah got into trouble for fighting in the cafeteria. She was suspended for that. This time, my tough buddy was walking with her head up, showing Riana and me that this wasn't going to be any big deal. I was already on punishment for our little mall excursion. The last thing I needed was one more reason for my parents to come down on me. I was scared.

As the librarian opened the office door, Riana and I were so hesitant about going in. The cute boots I had on would not move forward. Riana's dainty black pumps stood still as well.

"Come on, ladies, let's move," Mrs. Walsh said in a harsh way.

Layah didn't need any directions for the principal's office. She'd seen it many times before. Her Nikes kept walking. I could have fainted when we turned the corner by the copy machine. My mom was there. I had forgotten she was supposed to come up and volunteer.

My mom turned around toward the three of us and looked puzzled. "Ladies, what are you guys doing in the office?"

"Oh, everything is fine, Mrs. Browne," Layah said as she quickly gave my mom a hug.

Everything wasn't fine. And I certainly didn't need any extra drama by telling a fib on top of all of this. But before I could clear up the mess and tell the truth, my mom looked at the librarian, who wasn't smiling.

"No, ma'am, everything isn't all right. I'm bringing these three to see the principal. Is one of them your daughter?" Mrs. Walsh asked, trying to figure out which one of us belonged to my mother.

"Yes, this one right here," my mom said as she pulled my long pigtails. "My daughter is Carmen."

"The principal's ready to see you all now," the secretary said.

"I'll bring her in in just a second. I need a word with her. Is that okay?" my mom asked. Mrs. Walsh nodded and smiled approvingly. The way she looked at her was like she wanted my mom to give me a spanking or something.

Having my mom catch me going into the principal's office was way worse than me going to the principal's office without her seeing. This clearly was the worst day of my life. I'd brought it on myself, though.

"Before you say anything, Carmen, I want the truth. What's going on? Why in the world are you in the office?" my mom asked.

I told her exactly what happened. I took the blame. She knew that I tried to make my friends not do their work but laugh with me.

"I just don't understand that, Carmen Browne. You were supposed to be in the library doing research for your next paper. Not trying to stop your friends from working hard on theirs," my mom said, squeezing her hands into my shoulders.

I agreed. "I know, Mom. It was so easy to distract them. It was like I didn't even care about doing the work. And I hated that everybody was writing a paper but me. I don't know what I'm going to write on. I don't know what I'd do to change the world. I'm just ten years old."

My mom was listening. She wasn't getting mad. She was honestly trying to hear me out.

"And, Mom, I got an A on that last pressure. I mean, last paper. You see, Mom, I can't even get it out right. It's too much pressure," I said, defending why this was so hard for me.

"Nobody's demanding another A, sweetheart," she said as she gently placed her hand under my cheek. "Your father, your teacher, and I only want you to give your all. If that results in a grade less than an A, then we are happy with it. You have the ability to persuade people, evidenced by how you got your friends to follow you. So use those persuasive abilities to convince readers of your idea to change this world for the better."

I scratched my head. She was making a good point. Maybe I could do more than I thought I could.

"You can't be jealous of your friends just because they know what they want to write about. If you had your paper idea, you wouldn't want them to be mad at you. When you're working on your homework, you don't want any of us in the family to bother you. And a true friend wouldn't want to bring her friends down, but she'd be excited that her friends are doing something positive," my mom said again, making me understand what things about myself I needed to change. "Well, get on in there. I know the principal wants to talk to you."

"So I'm really in trouble now, huh?" I had to ask.

My mother turned me toward the principal's office

and said, "Talking to you, I think you feel worse than any punishment I or your father could give you."

"Sorry I let you down, Mom," I told her, glancing over my shoulder to look at her.

"Yeah, you really let me down in a big way. Here I am cutting out PTA reminder slips, and I see my own daughter in the office. It's like maybe I shouldn't be volunteering; maybe I should be at home waiting for you to get off the bus, so that I can stay more focused on you," she said as she shrugged her shoulders by the cutting board.

"No, Mom, I plan to do better," I said as she walked me into the principal's office.

★

When we walked into the fancy, mostly maroon office, I was shaking. Layah and Riana weren't grinning at all. My mom told Dr. Lamb that I had something to say. I admitted that I was the one who kept getting my friends in trouble. The principal admired my honesty and told my friends they could get back to class. Riana and Layah smiled at me. Dr. Lamb sat down and talked with my mom and me for another few minutes. Basically she said words that I took to heart.

"Carmen, it's okay to have high expectations for yourself, wanting to be a great student. When the creative stuff doesn't come as easily as it may come to others, that doesn't mean that it won't come in grand fashion when it comes. Do you understand what I'm saying?" Dr. Lamb questioned as she leaned forward from her desk.

I nodded. When I saw my mom from the corner of my eye, she was smiling, agreeing with Dr. Lamb.

"In other words, it's not the person who finishes a paper first but the quality and the thought behind the work." She stopped talking, but I knew there was something else she wanted to say.

"Yes, ma'am," I told her, biting my bottom lip.

She continued, "Your parents send you to school to get an education, not to get the class clown award. But because you came clean and I know you're new here . . . dealing with so many different things, trying to fit in, wearing new glasses, and just all the strings that fifth graders have to pull, this is a warning. But let me tell you, Miss Lady, there will be no more warnings. I will be watching you. I actually want to read your paper after you're done with it."

We talked a little while longer. She told me she used to go to school in my old hometown. Dr. Lamb was pretty cool once I got to know her. I didn't want to be in her office anymore, though.

"I'm actually proud to meet you. Your mom has been working in the office with me here. She's been a blessing to our PTA," Dr. Lamb said as she clapped her hands toward my mom. "She is going to help paint a mural for us on the school cafeteria wall. We certainly don't want her little girl in trouble. Do we?"

"No, ma'am," I said, a little nervous again.

"Good, then get on back with your class and strive to do your best." Dr. Lamb called someone. "I understand your class is not in the library anymore, so head to the classroom. You're a great student. Remember, you can do anything."

"Thanks, Dr. Lamb," I said as I got up to leave. "I won't let you down. And sorry again, Mom."

My mom nodded. As I walked back to my class, I held my head down. In a way, I was very relieved that I didn't have any school punishment or get my safety patrol belt swiped. God had looked out for me, only allowing me to get a warning. I held my head up when I realized it could have been a lot worse. My selfish actions had gotten my friends in trouble, and that wasn't cool.

Later, when we went to the cafeteria, I apologized to my two buddies. When they forgave me, I confessed that I really wished I knew what I was going to write about. So they prayed with me then and there that it would all come together soon. After that prayer, I believed it would all get worked out. I didn't know how, though, since the paper was due in a couple of weeks. I hadn't written one word.

★

Later that day, I thought about my talk with Dr. Lamb. She really believed in me. I felt better about finding something. However, I couldn't work on it because Clay came into my room to bother me with his problem.

"Hey, why don't you call this number," my brother said to me, handing me a phone number for Bethany Christian Services. "They are a Christian agency; certainly they've got to care."

"What do I tell them?" I asked, still really not wanting to do this.

"I don't know; you'll think of it. I'm looking on the Internet," Clay said, irritated. Our parents had safety controls on the computer and told us to always check with them before we went surfing on the Net. But I knew that Clay wouldn't say anything to them because he didn't want them to know what he was doing.

"I'm gonna find my parents, Carmen," Clay said confidently.

I had to go the kitchen to use the phone. Boy, was I nervous about being caught on the phone. Quickly dialing the number, I had no idea of what I would say when someone answered. I didn't want to be doing this anyway. However, since Clay said he really needed my help, I knew I had to do this or there would be another fallout.

"Bethany Christian Services," the sweet voice of the receptionist said into the receiver.

I hesitated, "I . . . umm, yeah . . . umm, may I speak with somebody that will help me with finding out something about adoption?"

"Yes, you sure can. Hold one second, please," the nice lady said to me.

"Okay, Lord," I said as I tapped my nail on the table, "speak for me."

Then an equally nice lady took my call. Her name was Martha Boston. She sounded like my grandmother.

"Hello, hello," she said into the receiver after she'd asked me to say something before. "Is someone there?"

Finally I piped up. "Yes, ma'am, I'm here."

I went on to tell her my name and briefly tell her why I was calling. She asked my age and I told her ten. After that she listened intently to the long version. When I was done explaining why this was so important to my brother to find his parents, she spoke.

She said, "I understand, but here is the law. In order for your brother to find out whom his parents are, he needs to be eighteen years old or have the approval of his adoptive parents. So, basically, I can't tell him anything because you said he's twelve and your parents think he needs to wait."

Hearing her words made me real sad for Clay. He wanted answers. This was like a dead end. I sighed in the phone.

"Ohhh, honey," Ms. Boston said, "Legally, sweetie, I can't help you find any information. There is nothing I can do on that front. But I will offer you some advice. Sounds like your brother doesn't think that adoption is a good thing. Based on all you've told me, it seems like he feels he is less of a person because he was adopted."

I said, "Yeah, that sounds right."

She continued, "Well, here's what I want you to talk to him about. Tell him he is not the only kid who has ever been adopted. Many children are in his position. He was blessed to have a family adopt him. There are thousands of kids in the custody of the state."

I asked her what that meant. She told me that being a ward of the state meant that kids who don't have parents have to either live with foster parents or at a group home. She then told me there are some who are with their parents who shouldn't be because their parents really aren't taking care of them. Those situations are called parental neglect, and that's when the Department of Children and Family Services, also known as DCFS, comes in to rescue kids.

"Tell Mr. Clay this would be a better world if there were more parents out there like yours who would adopt. We need more parents stepping out on faith and being a blessing to them," she said.

I sighed again. This time I felt relieved for Clay but sad for all the kids who didn't have parents. I never knew there were so many out there without folks to take care of them. My heart was aching.

Ms. Boston encouraged me to also talk to my mother. When I heard her coming around the corner, I quickly ended the call. Though I put the phone on the receiver, she knew I was doing something I wasn't supposed to.

"An explanation, young lady?" my mom asked as she headed to the freezer to take some meat out.

"Can I ask you a weird question?" I asked as she nodded her head and we both sat at the table. "Why did you guys really want to adopt?"

"I'm not sure why you asked, but I don't mind sharing. For me, being a Christian had a lot to do with it. I believe that God blessed your dad and me so that we could bless others. That's what adoption is all about. See, God adopted all of us into His family—those of us who accepted the fact that Jesus Christ is His Son. And the Lord gave us a passion to make a difference for a kid. I just want many more people to adopt little kids into their families. So many children are waiting and praying for a home," she said to me, sounding more genuine than her leather jacket I loved.

We talked more about adoption and waiting kids. She also told me she hoped Clay would come to embrace being in our family. We hugged and I told her I hoped that he would too.

Thinking about Clay really wanting to find his birth parents, I knew it might be tough for my brother to accept our family as enough. But I believed he was in the right place. He gets on my nerves a lot, but we love him so much.

"Well, you'd better get to your homework, and I've

got to get dinner started," my mom said. "How's that paper coming? You found a topic yet?"

Smiling from ear to ear I said, "Yep, now I know just what I would do to change the world."

"Carmen, that's great, what?" she asked in an impressed tone.

Excited I had a topic I loved, I said, "Mom, thanks to this talk, I know if I could change the world, I would make more people adopt so that no kid has to be alone."

"Well, I think that sounds like a wonderful topic. If you have any more questions, come to me and your dad."

She said she was proud of me for having such a good heart. And I felt better about talking to Clay. Though I had to give him bad news, overall the news was good. He had a family who loved him.

When I left the kitchen, Cassie was standing by the door. "Ooh, I'm going to tell Mama. I heard you on the phone. You're still working on the whole thing that they told y'all to leave alone."

"I said I'd do your chores," I jetted away from the kitchen.

"Yeah you said you would, but you haven't done any yet," she said, rolling her neck in my face.

We worked out a new agreement. The rest of the day, I spent cleaning her dirty room. Finally, after folding her clothes, putting away her socks, and placing many things in their right place, I thought I'd cleaned it good. Cassie, however, didn't agree. She wanted her shoes straightened, her bedsheets changed, and then all the toilets cleaned.

It was her turn to do the toilets. Some house chores were rotated and, boy, was I mad I had to clean these gross things again. I was tired. I had homework to do. I still needed to talk to Clay and tell him everything that Mrs. Boston and Mom had said to me.

Cassie had the nerve to come up and scream at me, even after I did all that. The little chump told me that I wasn't done. I walked around her and ignored the other words she said. I had already done too much. I had to go do my math and English. She got back in my face again and pushed my back. Oh, it was on then; I pushed her back. Then she pushed me again.

We were both screaming at the top of our voices. Not only had we forgotten the fact that we were inside, we had forgotten that our mom was home.

"I can't believe you don't understand that this is important to Clay," I shouted at her. "Plus, I'm trying to help him deal with it."

"You're not supposed to do what Mom and Dad told you not to do!" she screamed back.

"Yeah, but you're not supposed to be bribing me," I yelled.

She yanked my hair and said, "I don't even know what a bribe is."

"It's what you're holding over my head. I cleaned up

too much for you, and you still want me to do more." I grabbed her shirt so hard, she let my pigtail go.

I knew it wasn't right, me trying to help my brother when my parents told us to drop the whole adoption thing. He couldn't drop it and somebody had to help him. Why, why, why did my little sister have to find out what we were doing?

Why does life have to be so tough sometimes Lord? I thought to myself. So much was weighing me down. Cassie was making me sick. I had encouraging news for my brother that he may or may not find encouraging. And the fact that he couldn't let go of the whole adoption thing really got to me a lot more than I wanted to admit. Why couldn't he be happy with our family? And why didn't my parents understand the fact that he wasn't? If I could understand what my brother was going through, why couldn't my parents? I finally knew what I wanted to write about in my paper, but I couldn't even start my homework because of a pest called Cassie. *Help, Lord.*

I was crying. I was hurt and confused. Both of us were screaming at the top of our lungs at each other, and I knew we'd be in trouble soon. I'd been in so much trouble over the last couple of months; now I was sure to be in big trouble for fighting with my sister. My mom was bound to come from the kitchen and get on us because we were screaming. We weren't using an indoor voice.

8

Listen More

"What in the world is going on in here?" my mom yelled with a loud voice after she came barreling up the stairs.

She wasn't pleased to find my sister and me shouting back and forth at each other. I couldn't respond. I wasn't going to dare let Cassie get away with poking me. So, in front of my mom, I tagged her back. My mother demanded us to stop, and we knew we'd better or be in worse trouble. Clay rushed in to see what was up.

"What's goin' on with y'all?" Clay said, puzzled.

"They obviously have forgotten who they are," my mom said, disgusted.

Then we heard the sound that made us

instantly pull apart. It was the garage door going up. That could only be one person. Dad. I didn't have to tell Cassie to let go, nor did she have to say anything to me. We just froze.

"Naw, don't look like that now that your dad is home," my mother said, staring us down.

My mom then had one hand on her hip and the other on her head as if she were about to faint. She paced back and forth. If steam really could come out of people's ears when they got mad, my mom would have some coming out of her ears right now.

"Clay, go and get your dad," she said in a harsh tone.

"No, Mom," Cassie pleaded, pulling on my mom's shirt. "Please, Mom, we're sorry."

My mother shook her head at my sister. I had my arms folded and completely looked away. I didn't want her to tell my dad, but I wasn't sorry either, because my sister was a brat. If she needed to get in trouble to calm down and I had to get in trouble with her, then that's just what was going to have to happen, because I wasn't sorry.

"What is going on up here?" my dad asked, rushing into my room. "Clay comes running out to the car. I'm not even parked. He's saying it's some emergency. The girls are fighting up here."

As mad as I'd been at Cassie, it didn't even compare to how mad my daddy was with the two of us. This wasn't good. Cassie and I both tried to explain.

Wiping his eyebrows, he said, "Hush, hush and listen.

That's your problem; you think you know everything. When I want you guys to speak, I'll ask you to say something. Right now I am just completely disappointed that you guys were fighting."

He walked over to my mom, with her arms folded. She unfolded them and gave him a kiss. I hoped that move would soften him. However, he put his hand on my purple wall and breathed hard.

"Honey, what's going on?" he asked my mom.

"I don't know what's wrong with them, Charles."

I thought to myself, *Dad, if you'd listen we're trying to tell you what's going on.* Of course, I kept my cool and remembered to whom I was about to say something smart. So I said nothing.

Cassie ran over to Mom and didn't stay quiet like Dad told us. "It was all her fault, Mom. She and Clay have been going behind you and Dad's back, trying to find out who his real parents are."

I didn't believe my dad's angered face could get any more upset, but it did. "What?"

Clay tried to take a few steps out the door. My dad touched his shoulder and sorta dragged him back into my room. I wanted to hide in my closet.

"Wait a minute, Son. Is what Cassie said true?"

Clay confirmed it and then dropped his head. My mother just started crying. Daddy headed over to her and took her hand.

"Honey, calm down. It's okay." Daddy wiped her eyes

with his free hand and then turned back to Cassie. "What does that have to do with you and your sister fighting, though?"

"'Cause of them," she said, pointing at Clay and me.

My dad came over to me. I didn't know what was about to happen next. I knew deep down that fighting with Cassie was wrong.

He said, "This adoption thing is a whole other issue. I'll deal with that in a bit. You and your sister fighting is not acceptable, Carmen."

I looked at my brother and shrugged my shoulders. I hated to have to tell the whole truth because that might hurt my brother. My dad had asked, though. It left me with no choice but to come clean. Thankfully, my brother gave me the go-ahead look. That meant we'd still be cool. Clay understood.

"Okay, Dad, she's right," I said to my father. "I did agree to help Clay. But I'm sorry for going behind your back."

Staring at Clay harshly he said, "Well, that's what it was. We told your brother to leave it alone, and we certainly knew everybody in the house heard us." Dad shook his head in disappointment at me. "That meant you too. Both of you guys know better than to do something that I said no to. Again, though, what does that have to do with you and your sister fighting?"

"Well, she found out that I was trying to help him and . . . ," I said before slowing down.

"What?" Mom said furiously.

Cassie bragged, "And so I wouldn't tell, she offered to do some of my chores."

"Carmen, you bribed your sister?" she asked, hoping my answer would be no.

My mom made what I did sound so bad. Though I didn't pay her off with money, I did pay her off with my service. My mom waited for my honest answer.

"Yes, Mom, I guess I did. I shouldn't even say I'm sorry, though," I defended, feeling I did the right thing.

Mom said, "Actually, Carmen, I don't even want to hear an apology. You've been saying sorry for so much lately. Over the last couple of months you've really acted out of character. Saying sorry wouldn't even cut it for me as an explanation this time."

"Okay, it's like this, Mom and Dad. Clay's been upset. He's been really upset about his parents, and you guys haven't been hearing him. You just tell him to forget it and I told him to forget it too, but he couldn't forget it. I mean, he's been really sad lately and he asked for my help. I didn't want to help him, but I felt he might run away if no one here was on his side. So I helped."

My parent's expressions were hard to read. I couldn't tell what they were thinking. I didn't want him to run away, though.

I explained. "I remember when we had to move here, and nobody understood how I felt. So I ran away. I just went down the street to Jillian's house, and you guys found me. I later learned that my decision was stupid to run away. I learned my lesson. But I didn't want Clay to leave and find out the hard way. Or, worse, run away to a place where we couldn't find him. So I helped him." I said that in a little softer voice.

My dad twitched his mouth and then said, "Let me get this straight: You helped your brother try to find his parents, and your sister found out about it. Since she knew we didn't want you to do that, she said she was going to tell. To keep her quiet you decided to do some of her chores?"

"Yep." I nodded my head. "That's correct."

My mother added, "I can see what happened next. Cassie wanted you to do too many chores, and that's when you guys went at each other."

Though she didn't ask a question, both Cassie and I had to respond. We nodded on that one. My mom knew us well.

"Cassie, if there's ever something that you think your mom and I need to know, you tell us and we'll handle it," my dad said.

"You don't take matters into your own hands and pressure other people. Do you understand me?" my mom asked, irritated at her as well.

"Yes, Mommy," Cassie said as she went to give my mom a hug.

My dad plopped on my bed. He held his face in his arms. I was across the room leaning on my closet door.

Clay was standing in the doorway. My dad didn't appear happy with Clay or me.

"You're not mad at me, Dad?" I looked over and asked.

My mom came up to me and let out her tears. "How could we be mad at you, baby? You were just trying to help your brother."

She hugged me tight. I was happy to get her affection. I wanted my dad to say he wasn't mad, but he didn't.

"So what did you guys find out?" my dad said instead as he stood to his feet and folded his arms.

I went on to tell everyone that we came up with an empty search. I told them that since Clay wasn't eighteen, no one would give him any information. That he needed his parents' help to find his birth parents. My brother, heartbroken, hung his head.

I was sad for Clay, realizing that he might never know his birth parents. When he kicked my door, I wished I had better information for him. I so wanted to tell him he was blessed to have us, but it didn't seem like those words would matter.

My dad's eyes watered as he watched Clay. "You want to know about your parents, Son? Sorry we didn't listen. We'll tell you. You guys get ready to wash up for dinner. We'll talk about this later tonight."

My dad patted Clay on the bottom and then left my crowded room. My mother hugged my brother and then she left. Clay clasped his hands up toward heaven and then told me thanks before he went to the bathroom. His exit left only Cassie and me.

"Sorry, Carmen," my little sister said to me in a voice that sounded sincere. "You were just trying to help Clay. I guess I made it worse, huh?"

I went and placed my arm around my sister. "It's okay, Sis. At least now Mom and Dad are going to tell him everything."

Clay popped his head back into my doorway. "You're like a little hero, Cassie. Both of you guys are, really. I'm just sorry I had you fighting over this." Clay came over to us. We all hugged and it was really cool. He was happy, and I was happy for him.

★

Later that night, my parents sat us down in the family room. They were holding hands and the three of us sat across from them. This really serious discussion we were about to have seemed like it wasn't going to be easy for them.

Actually, it wasn't gonna be easy for me either. Though the topic of Clay's other family was what I knew we were going to discuss, I wasn't ready to talk about it. I just sat there and waited for my parents to speak. Clay and Cassie did the same.

Gripping my mom's hand tighter, Dad held out some papers. He gestured for Clay to come and get them. My brother slowly walked across the room, grabbed the crumbled-up white documents, and sat back down beside me. Cassie peered over his shoulder and tried to read. She was in the third grade and she could read well, but she always read out loud. Her way was real annoying.

Clay kinda folded the paper over his way and said to her, "May I read it first, please?"

"Cassie, get back, but, Clay, wait," my dad said.

"Let's pray first," dad said. "Lord, we ask for Your help and Your strength in handling this situation. Thank You for each of our children. We know that Your Word says that we are fearfully and wonderfully made. You love them more than we ever could. We want to be better parents who reflect Your love to our children. We trust You for victory in our lives. In Jesus' name, we pray. Amen.

"Son, it's only three pages and it's not really much. It does state what your name used to be, date of birth, and legal status. It also goes into some birth and development information, psychological stuff that they knew about you at age three, and physical description information on your birth parents. The last thing there is what they recommended for you."

My mom's eyes were so red and watery, she could barely look up at the three of us. I knew her heart was breaking as if someone were taking her child away. Nobody was taking Clay away, but he wanted to go and I think that's what made her really sad. And for the first time it seemed like Clay could see that.

After Clay looked at my mom he said under his breath, "Wow, she's really hurt."

The way our mom felt about her son was showing in her body language. She couldn't keep her legs still, her eyes watered even more, and she was sweating a lot.

Then my dad kissed her on the cheek and said, "It's okay. He just wants to know, honey."

"But I want him to want to be with us," she finally broke down and said.

My dad could only look away. Clay bit his lip. My sister went over and hugged Mom. I couldn't move. I was numb. I wanted this thing to be over, but I knew we had to do this for Clay.

Also, I wanted to know what kind of people could leave their baby. It just didn't seem right. I wanted an explanation.

"Dad, tell us what you know," I said as if I were Clay.

Dad went on to tell us that he wanted to give this information to Clay much, much later in his life, but since he was insistent he went on and shared. Since he didn't want Cassie and I to get the wrong information, he and my mom agreed to tell all three of us.

His father was listed as unknown on his birth certificate. After further investigation no father was identified. Clay had two biological half brothers and no sisters. His mom was a young lady who didn't feel that she could adequately take care of another baby. The other brothers were older than Clay.

"Do you know where my brothers are?" Clay asked my dad, as he stayed strong.

"I don't, Son. But the agency can get us that information if you like," my dad said.

Clay just sat there looking stunned.

My dad left my mom and came over to my brother. "Clay, what we do know is that the mom and dad standing before you want to help you get through life. We want you more than you know, Son. And no other parents could love any of their children more than we love the three of you. Birth child, first child, adopted child, youngest child, middle child, girl child, boy child, it doesn't matter, and I even love fighting children." He smiled at me. "Our love is unconditional. God placed it in our hearts. Honestly, I never saw myself adopting anybody's kids. I didn't see how I could feel the same, but God worked all that out. Just how He used adopting me to be one of His kids and loves me more than I can understand, that's how I love you, Clay. And you know I love your sisters no different. You know I'd give my life for all of you. I love you."

Clay looked up at Daddy and hugged his waist so hard. "Dad, I love you too."

My mom was holding my sister and they were crying. I squeezed my hands together and thanked God. He had listened to all of our prayers. He was fixing my family.

Clay left my dad and went over to Mom and said, "I'm sorry for making you think that I wanted something more."

"After finally hearing you out, I understand, Clay," she said as she stood up and hugged her big baby.

We weren't the family he was on a mission to look for, but I could tell he was so happy that we were the family that he found. My dad motioned for Cassie and me to come to his arms. As Dad hugged us both, we all felt loved, and that felt good.

✪

"Okay, okay, I hear y'all," I said to my two girlfriends as we practiced our song for the talent show. "You don't want to sing a gospel song."

"No, no, it's not that we don't want to sing about God or anything," Riana tried unsuccessfully to convince me. "It's just that this is school. Can we sing something with a little bit of juice?"

"What are you saying? Gospel songs aren't fun?" I took offense and said.

"We can't even pray in school," Layah said.

"So we can't be disqualified or nothing because we were told we could sing whatever we wanted," I argued back.

It didn't matter what I kept saying. They wanted to do it their way or they didn't want to sing with me. Compromising wasn't so bad.

Listening to what my friends wanted, I was bummed out that they didn't want to sing a gospel song. But then I was comforted in thinking that every time I opened my mouth—as long as I made God proud—it'd be good. Even though I was still a little mad with my friends that they didn't want to do it my way, they had agreed to come with me that night to church for a Sounds Unlimited concert.

Sounds Unlimited was such a talented group. It was about twenty people that were in high school or college or around that age. Their songs had such great beats. Both of my friends looked at me and had to eat their words. All Christian songs weren't boring or lame. We got up and praised and danced with everybody else in the place.

My dad was there as well, with a lot of his football players to support someone performing in the concert. Since it was the off-season, the players had been helping with recruiting, training, and spending time in the weight room. They had a lot of time to get to know the new members of the staff, not just my dad as head coach but Snake too. My dad hired him to do something called strength and conditioning.

He tried to explain it to me, but all I knew was that it was the person who helped players lift weights and stuff. Even though I knew Snake was cool, it was still kinda scary remembering seeing the three of those dudes in the backwoods who scared us when we first moved here. Snake ended up being a really great person to know, and when he opened his mouth and started rapping a hip-hop Bible story, I wanted to hear more. Then when the choir came in behind him on the chorus, I wanted to sing with them.

"Thank you all," Snake said from the mic. "Before I sing my last song, I want to give a little testimony. My life has really been hard. I never knew who my dad was; my mom was addicted to this or that all my life growing up; I pretty much raised her. And what did a kid know, you know? I just knew about working out and bustin' rhythms. Recently I got saved. I needed to grow closer to God. I prayed about God showing me someone who could teach me more about His Word. 'Cause sometimes it was just too hard for me to understand, and then He sent Coach Browne my way. His mentoring me has made me a better Christian."

I looked back at my dad and he had such a big smile on his face. Hearing Snake talk about my dad so positively made me smile too. The Brownes were proud of him.

"He has taken me under his wing, not only giving me a job, but he's listened to my problems. He's prayed with me and given me some direction and hope. He's shown me what a walk with God is really supposed to be about. He's been like a father not only to me but also to a lot of the guys on the team, and he's just gotten here. Most of the time people see my toughness, and they judge me negatively. Coach Browne didn't do that, though. He really listened to what I had to say instead of telling me what he thought I should be and what I should think," Snake continued as he found my dad in the crowd. "Thanks, sir."

My strong dad was misty-eyed. Clay was sitting beside him, and he looked proud of his father. The song Snake sung was a slow, rapping tune, which he dedicated to my dad. Just like the title, "Listen Up," the words told how to really grow closer to people. Before we can pray for them, we've got to listen to them. We can't just talk all the time and hear just a piece of what they say. Or maybe not even hear them at all. In order to truly connect with people, we've got to listen more.

9

Simply Right

I surprised myself at how much I'd learned, even though it was a tough lesson. I'd gotten in trouble a lot this semester. It felt good that it wasn't all for nothing. I was growing.

As we sat in our seats the principal came on the intercom and said, "Teachers, please pardon the interruption. Due to the low number of entries this year, the talent show will be canceled. However, we are asking those who did sign up to sing at our PTA meeting next month for exhibition. Thank you."

Layah, Riana, and I just looked at each other with sad faces. All the practicing we'd done, all the work we'd done. Not cool at all. My teacher noticed we didn't look happy.

She came over to us since we all sat in a row and said, "I know you ladies are very competitive. I watch you out there on the blacktop, and even with your grades you guys are natural competitors, but singing comes from the heart. You don't always have to sing to win a prize. You sing to encourage people. You should strive to do it to give a message from your songs. So don't get discouraged. Keep on practicing so you can show off at the PTA, all right?"

She lifted her hand into the air for us to slap it. She was cool. She told us what we needed to hear. We nodded.

✪

Saturday morning my mom had me cleaning the house to get ready for company. I didn't know much of what was going on. However, to make up for all the trouble I had gotten in, I did all the chores and even picked up in some extra places that were supposed to be my brother's and sister's responsibilities just to make the house look extra special.

It'd be our first time this spring grilling. Boy, did I like char-grilled hotdogs. The more burnt they were, the better they tasted to me.

First, Snake and his crew pulled up. I was really surprised to see them. I knew Snake worked with my dad, but now he was at our house for a cookout. Clay was happy, though. He'd helped them set up their stereo and turntable downstairs.

"What's going on?" I asked my mom as she whipped up a salad.

"It's a surprise, honey," she said, winking at me.

Just then the doorbell rang again. I skipped over a bunch of stairs and opened it.

I was so surprised to see one of the girls, Bianca, from Pure Grace, the girl group I sang with in D.C. It was she and my dad's friend who owned a record company, and his wife.

"Hey, little songbird," Bianca said to me. "I've got a cool surprise for you."

It turned out to be so cool. She played a song that I was singing background on. At one point, they played my voice only in the song with my parents' permission, of course. I was sorta featured on it and it was the bomb. The song was called, "God Is Watching." I loved it. I went over and hugged Bianca so hard.

Then Bianca and I had such great girl talk. I told her all about my lesson that I'd learned on not telling the truth. And I told her about how my singing group was coming. She smiled and told me to keep on working at it. I was already on my way. Bianca told me she had never recorded anything until she was in college. Here I was in the fifth grade and on their album.

Later, after we ate, another great surprise happened. Turns out that my dad invited Snake and his friends to perform for his buddy. I thought Snake was good at the church the other night, but he was even better right now.

He was able to give a mini concert, like seven songs. And not only did my dad's friend like it, he wanted to sign them. Snake was given a contract on the spot. We were all so excited for Snake and his boys.

Snake said, "Coach Browne, I could never thank you enough, man."

My dad responded, "Once is thanks enough. Besides, now it looks like I might lose my best assistant strength coach. Don't sign him, Tim," my dad said, laughing.

"Oh, don't worry," my dad's old teammate said "You know the music business takes a minute. We'll be able to share his time."

"Cool," my dad laughed and said. "For real, Snake, if I have to lose you to your dream, it's all good. I know your life has been tough, but that's why you never give up. You always have to do the right thing. You always need to help others 'cause what you give comes back. It says in His Word, 'When you do it to the least of them, you do it to Me also.' You've been a blessing, and now God is rewarding you. You kept it real and now you got a real contract in your hand."

My father and Snake slapped hands and embraced.

"Your son and I have been talking," Snake said as he motioned for Clay to come over to him. "We talked about his feeling a little bad that he was adopted."

"Yeah, we just came through a pretty rough time," my dad said.

Snake replied, "Like I told Clay, I kinda wished I was

adopted. My mom was so busy trying to do illegal stuff that she couldn't even be a mom. Nobody told on my mom. And nobody cared enough to tell anybody that I wasn't being looked after, so I had to raise myself. My only wish was that I could have had different parents. You know, somebody to be there for me. And even somebody to take me in. Somebody to raise me as if I was their own."

My dad nodded. Snake had a hard life. This contract was what he needed. Clay stood next to our dad.

Clay said, "I'm glad I found out that I'm really blessed. I knew it the other day, but I know it even more now after talking to Snake. Thank you, Dad, thank you. I'll never think about my other family again. This is the only one I need."

"Well, Son, I learned something as well. It's okay to remember your past. Maybe I was wrong for wanting you not to think about it. It's a part of who you are. Just know that everybody in this world has shortcomings. None of us is going to be perfect until we get to heaven. So if you ever want to talk about your family, or if you ever want to reach out to your brothers, you just come talk to me, and we'll figure out what's best together. Sound good?"

"Sounds real good," Clay said.

The rest of the evening was totally tight. We ate more barbecue and Mom's potato salad. We also sat around and had a mini talent show. Of course, with Bianca's great voice and Snake's cool rap it was tough to beat.

✪

School would be out in a few weeks, and it seemed like the second semester just went so fast. I always thought I couldn't wait until middle school, but now I was becoming a little sad that I would be leaving elementary. But when I thought about it, I knew next year I would be ready. Yeah, I didn't have it all figured out, but heading into middle school, I knew that as long as I remembered to tell the truth and be the kind of friend I wanted people to be to me, with God on my side I could get through anything.

So I looked over at my teddy bear Budgie that had been my buddy for years. I knew it was time for me to grow up. I used to not be able to sleep if he wasn't near. However, I hadn't talked to him since the first night my sister found him.

Picking him up off my bed and placing him on a shelf I said, "Bye Budgie, I think I can take it from here now. But watch out for me from on high."

Yep, I could honestly say I was growing up.

✪

A week later the papers were posted. I couldn't believe it, but I'd gotten a hundred again. My grade was the highest in the class. So not only at the PTA would I have to sing, but I'd have to recite my paper too. Man, all that getting upset for nothing. I had it in me. As always, the teacher sent home the top three papers in her newsletter. This time my mom and I sat down and read it together.

She was so proud of me. I had given my best. Then I told her that I was proud of her. She was such a great mom, and I knew because of that we'd be closer.

The third-place entry read:

If I could change the world I would make it so guys wouldn't like girls. I know that sounds a little harsh, but I really do feel that way. I'm only in the fifth grade and I like this girl. However, ever since my friends found out they've been picking on me. I can handle their jokes here and there, but I got mad at the girl because I thought she was the one that told the world. I learned that wasn't the case. Though I've apologized, she hardly talks to me anymore. That bothers me.

So back to my point, if I could change the world I'd make it so guys don't like girls. Then I'd never like her in the first place and it really wouldn't hurt my feelings that she doesn't talk to me anymore. Even though that would help me now, maybe my idea to change the world isn't really a good one. Then my dad wouldn't like my mom. My grandparents wouldn't be married and I guess maybe one day I'd want to like a girl too. Actually, I still like this one. So to sum it up, I think the world is cool just the way it is.

–William Spencer

The second-place entry read:

> If I could change the world, I'd make it so that every-
> one would tell the truth. The last couple of months, I've
> learned so much from telling lies. I really got myself into a
> lot of trouble. I got stuck in a snowstorm because of it too.
> Yep, I found stretching the truth or just plain not trying to
> tell the truth at all, isn't the way to go. It hurts people and
> most of the time it's a cover up for something else. If peo-
> ple could just be honest with themselves they'd find a way
> to deal with whatever is really going on.
>
> A good friend told me this advice. I tried it and it
> worked. I didn't get my way with what I wanted, but I'm
> closer to my mom because I opened up. We talked about
> my problems. Going behind her back and lying is not
> right. More people need to tell the truth. If we all did that,
> the world would be a better place.
>
> —Riana Anderson

Lastly, my first-place entry read:

> If I could change the world, I'd have more families
> open up their homes for kids who didn't have one. I'm
> talking about adoption. I never thought that my adopted
> brother didn't belong in my family, but he had problems
> with it. So I went on a search to help him find his birth
> family.
>
> In doing so, I learned so much about all the kids who
> are in foster care, in group homes, or in abusive situations

with their real families. Finding out all that helped me see that if people just stepped out on faith and tried to give a little of their blessing to somebody else, they would give kids with no hope, hope. Not only would they find that the kids would be blessed, but, trust me, that family would be blessed even more. All of us want someone to love and accept us. Adoption can help a kid who's been rejected feel accepted. Yep, people need to adopt. I'm so happy my family did. We truly found out it's a wonderful thing and our world is better off. Adoption isn't wrong; it's simply right.

—Carmen Browne